The Sonic Breach

Read all the books in the
**TOM SWIFT INVENTORS'
ACADEMY** series!

The Drone Pursuit
The Sonic Breach

TOM SWIFT

INVENTORS' ACADEMY

-BOOK 2-
The Sonic Breach

VICTOR APPLETON

Aladdin
NEW YORK LONDON TORONTO SYDNEY NEW DELHI

ALADDIN

An imprint of Simon & Schuster Children's Publishing Division
1230 Avenue of the Americas, New York, New York 10020
First Aladdin hardcover edition July 2019
Text copyright © 2019 by Victor Appleton
Jacket illustration copyright © 2019 by Kevin Keele
TOM SWIFT and related marks are trademarks of Simon & Schuster, Inc.
Also available in an Aladdin paperback edition.
All rights reserved, including the right of reproduction in whole or in part in any form.
ALADDIN and related logo are registered trademarks of Simon & Schuster, Inc.
For information about special discounts for bulk purchases, please contact
Simon & Schuster Special Sales at 1-866-506-1949 or business@simonandschuster.com.
The Simon & Schuster Speakers Bureau can bring authors to your live event.
For more information or to book an event contact the Simon & Schuster Speakers Bureau
at 1-866-248-3049 or visit our website at www.simonspeakers.com.
Jacket designed by Heather Palisi-Reyes
Interior designed by Mike Rosamilia
The text of this book was set in Adobe Caslon Pro.
Manufactured in the United States of America 0519 FFG
10 9 8 7 6 5 4 3 2 1
Library of Congress Cataloging-in-Publication Data
Names: Appleton, Victor, author.
Title: The sonic breach / by Victor Appleton.
Description: First Aladdin hardcover/paperback edition. | New York : Aladdin, 2019. |
Series: Tom Swift Inventors' Academy ; #2 | Summary: When someone steals an "app" that
Amy wrote and profits from it, Tom and his friends use a robot to help catch the thief.
Identifiers: LCCN 2018036998 (print) | LCCN 2018042126 (eBook) | ISBN 9781534436350
(eBook) | ISBN 9781534436336 (pbk) | ISBN 9781534436343 (hc)
Subjects: | CYAC: Inventors—Fiction. | Hackers—Fiction. | Stealing—Fiction. |
Robots—Fiction. | Schools—Fiction. | Friendship—Fiction. | Science fiction.
Classification: LCC PZ7.A652 (eBook) | LCC PZ7.A652 Mos 2019 (print) |
DDC [Fic]—dc23
LC record available at https://lccn.loc.gov/2018036998

Contents

1

The Conjunction
Malfunction

"YOU'RE GOING DOWN, WATTS," NOAH SAID TO
his opponent.

"Bring it, Newton," Jamal Watts replied.

The two faced off inside a circle of other students.
And no, this wasn't some kind of after-school fight. It
wasn't even after school. This was during our robotics
class, and the two combatants weren't combatants at all.
A large robot rested on the floor beside each of them.

One of the cool things about attending the Swift
Academy of Science and Technology is that you never
knew what the day might have in store. Sure, most

1

schools held field trips to local museums, but Swift Academy students may get to work on a project with NASA. Regular schools might have well-equipped science departments. But the academy students have access to a lot of the high-end equipment at the next-door Swift Enterprises—a major government contractor.

Or, we could keep it simple like today and have a robot battle sparring session in part of the gym during robotics. All right, there were several cool things about our school.

"Okay, teams," Mrs. Scott said with a smirk as she strolled to the center of the circle. Her usual red bandanna held back her curly jet-black hair. Usually dressed in overalls, she always looked like someone who grew up in a mechanics shop. And judging by the wrench tattoo peeking out from her rolled up shirtsleeve, she probably was. "Enough trash talk. Final checks."

This year, Mrs. Scott had us build robots for our very own robot battle—just like the ones you see on television. She had outlined the specifications for the robots and we divided into teams to build one of our own. Luckily, I got to work with my friends Noah Newton and Samantha Watson.

Noah worked the joysticks on his controller. Our robot's body was half a meter square and fifteen centimeters tall. It looked like an oversize flat gift box painted battleship gray. The robot moved forward and backward as Noah controlled it. "Locomotion, check," he said.

Sam toggled the joysticks on her controller. She was in charge of the three axes protruding from the top of our robot—two in the front, one in the back. Okay, they weren't real axes—more like ax-shaped hammers with blunt edges. But I designed the heads to be shaped in such a way that they created a ramp when the front two were in the down position; the same with the one on the back. That way, our robot could not only whack an opposing robot but also wedge itself underneath the opponent. Then the axes could raise and potentially flip over the enemy.

"Axes are a go," Sam reported as the ax heads raised and lowered. Even though we had only plastic heads installed for today's practice match, a devious grin stretched across her face as she brought them down in a chopping motion.

My job was a little different. I had a tablet connected to my controller for power distribution. Noah had coded a simplistic AI for our robot. It wasn't a true artificial intelligence, but it stored several preset maneuvers. It also allowed power levels to be adjusted in real time. With a swipe on my tablet, I could give more power to the axes for attacks or flips. I could also assign all power to the drive motor for a quick escape.

I checked the readings on the tablet. "AI and power levels are good," I announced.

Noah turned to me and grinned. "One final test," he said, his dark eyes gleaming through his safety goggles. "Let's hear it, Tom."

"Really?" I asked. "For a practice match?"

"Come on," Noah urged. "You know you want to."

Noah had pulled the team leader card and insisted on naming our robot. He called it the Choppa. That made sense and all; it did wield three ax-shape hammers. But the real reason behind the name was a meme he had found on the Internet. It showed a picture of Arnold Schwarzenegger standing in a jungle, muscles rippling and covered in sweat and camouflage face paint. Under the image were the words *GET TO THE CHOPPA!* Noah liked the meme so much that he talked us into pasting the image on the top of our robot.

"Come on! Do it!" Noah growled in his best Arnold impersonation. "Do it! I'm right here!"

I shook my head and pressed a button on my controller.

"Get to za choppa!" shouted Arnold's voice from a hidden speaker on our robot. "Get to za choppa!"

The surrounding students laughed. Nothing cracks up a bunch of twelve- and thirteen-year-olds like a good meme, even an oldie but a goody.

Our opposing team readied their robot. The team consisted of Jamal Watts, Maggie Ortiz, and Tony Garret. Their robot was called Flailing Grade. It was about the same size as ours but it was completely round. It was able to spin really fast and, thanks to some clever programming by Jamal, it was also able to maneuver around while it spun. However, it got its name because it wielded a small flail as it spun—you know, that medieval weapon with the metal ball at the end of a long chain, dangling from a stick.

Flailing Grade didn't have its little metal wrecking ball at the moment. Instead, a red foam ball hung from the end of its chain. A safety precaution just like the Choppa's rigid plastic ax heads. This was just sparring practice, after all, meant to get the feel of squaring off against a real opponent. Not to cause actual damage before the real battle. That's also why all the students simply watched from a wide circle around the robots.

In the upcoming robot battle, Mrs. Scott had arranged to have the entire gym converted into a mini robot battle arena. The wooden floor would be covered and the audience and controllers would be safe behind thick, clear plastic sheeting. I knew she couldn't pull off rows of saw blades slicing up from the floor or pits with erupting flames like some of the TV shows. But it was going to be exciting nonetheless.

"All right, are both teams ready?" asked Mrs. Scott.

"Ready," replied Noah.

"We're ready," Jamal announced.

I glanced at my tablet for the third time. This was our team's first practice match so I was a bit nervous.

Mrs. Scott raised a hand. "Three! Two! One! Battle!" She ran out from between the robots.

I diverted all power to the main motor as the Choppa sped toward Flailing Grade. The yellow robot moved away from us as it began to spin. The thing about spinning robots is that they take a while to get up to full speed. If it had attacked us immediately, its flail, metal or not, wouldn't have enough momentum to deliver a damaging blow. That's why we had to move in as fast as possible. Unfortunately, Tony's team did a great job at staying out of reach.

We didn't give up. Noah kept at it, closing the gap between the two robots. "Get ready, Sam," Noah said.

Just then, out of the corner of my eye, I spotted a figure dressed in all white, jogging up to me. A quick glance told me it was someone wearing a fencing uniform. Our robotics class only took up part of the gym. The fencing team practiced on the other end.

"Did I miss anything?" asked a familiar voice.

"We just started," I replied. My eyes flicked back and forth from my tablet to the two robots.

Amy Hsu removed her mask and leaned closer. Her black hair was pulled back into a ponytail. She was a close friend and the final member of the Formidable Foursome, as my dad called us.

"Wow," she said. Then she poked my shoulder. "Do the thing."

Not taking my eyes off the power levels, I tapped the button on my controller.

"Get to za Choppa!" shouted our robot.

Amy chuckled. "That kills me."

Flailing Grade was not up to maximum speed when the Choppa finally caught up to it. However, the foam ball bounced off the side of our robot and several students clapped.

"Glancing blow," Mrs. Scott reported.

Sam worked the joysticks and both front ax heads raised. When our robot was in position, I slid my fingers across the screen, diverting power to the axes. Sam made them slam down atop Flailing Grade. More students applauded. Some cheered.

"Solid hit," said Mrs. Scott.

The plastic heads weren't enough to stop the other robot's momentum completely, but they slowed it down a bit. Still Noah pulled back the joysticks, dodging the foam flail as it came back around.

"Let's go for a flip," said Noah. "You with me, team?"

"Oh yeah!" said Sam. She pulled down on the joysticks, and the ax heads lowered to their bottom position.

"I'm ready," I replied as I redistributed the power back to the main drive motor. "If you time it just right . . ."

"We can dodge the flail," Noah finished, edging our robot closer. "Who's driving this thing, anyway?"

I shrugged. "Just saying."

"Teamwork, guys," Sam scolded, never dropping her gaze from the two robots. "Less talking, more flipping."

Noah edged our robot closer. The flail swung by once, twice, three times. When it passed again, Noah jammed the joysticks forward. The tips of the axes slid under the other robot, tilting it off the ground. With the enemy robot askew, the flail came back around and whizzed harmlessly above the Choppa.

"That's right," Noah said as he kept the momentum going. He pushed Flailing Grade forward, not letting it get traction.

I used two fingers to swipe the tablet, sending all power to the front axes. "Now, Sam!"

Sam jammed the joysticks forward and our axes shot up, launching Flailing Grade into the air.

All the spectators cheered as the yellow robot shot straight up.

"Yes!" I shouted.

My eyes widened and the crowd's cheers quickly turned to groans when Flailing Grade fell straight down and landed atop the Choppa. I cringed as the rear plastic ax head snapped off.

"No way," said Sam.

"Great flip," Mrs. Scott announced. "But a self-inflicted hit by the Choppa." Some of the students laughed.

I shook my head in disgust. The biggest hit of the match was one we'd given ourselves.

Lucky for Jamal's team, Flailing Grade landed right side up. It began to spin again.

"Get to za Choppa!" our robot shouted.

Noah glanced at me. "Not now, dude!"

I glanced at my controller. "Uh, I didn't do that."

Noah went back to his controller. He jerked the joysticks up and down and our robot moved in stuttering arcs inside the circle. "I . . . think we have a problem."

"What's it doing?" asked Amy.

"I don't know," I replied, looking at my tablet. "I think it's cycling through the presets."

The axes began moving up and down. Even the now-empty metal rod on the back acted as if it were chopping with an invisible ax head.

"Okay, I'm not doing that," said Sam.

"That's the problem." Noah's brow furrowed as he worked the joysticks. "I've lost control."

"Get to za choppa!" our robot repeated. "Get to za choppa!"

I groaned. "That last hit must've damaged the motherboard. I'm killing the power."

I slid all three power bars to zero. It had no effect. The robot continued to move forward and back in jerky motions. The axes chopped air.

Noah glanced back at me. "You going to do it anytime soon?"

I slid the powers up to full and back down to zero. Nothing happened. "I'm trying." I shook my head. "I'm locked out too."

The audience had been laughing at our robot's crazy movements. But then they cheered when Flailing Grade swooped in and laid into us with its flail.

Bap-bap-bap-bap-bap!

"Multiple hits," said Mrs. Scott.

"Aw, man!" I said, flinching with every hit. In a real match, that might've sent our robot reeling. "You getting anything?" I asked Noah.

"Nothing!" Noah banged the side of his controller with one hand. "Come on!" he growled.

"Get to za Choppa! Get to za Choppa!" our robot repeated.

"Wow," Sam said, struggling with her own controller. "That's not so funny anymore."

Then our robot stopped its stuttering movements and took off in a straight line. Students jumped out of the way as it raced out of the circle. Noah, Sam, and I chased after it, each of us still working our controls.

"Go for the kill switch!" I shouted.

Mrs. Scott had us install a switch in the back of each robot in case something like this happened. The trouble was getting to the thing while the robot sped across the gym floor.

"I'll get it when it hits the wall," Noah said between breaths.

The robot veered left and right as it moved. It blared "Get to za Choppa!" all the way as it neared the wall.

"It's not going to, is it?" asked Sam.

"It looks like it," I replied.

The robot veered toward the open doorway.

"Ah, man!" Noah shouted as he led the way.

The Choppa zipped out of the gym and disappeared around the corner beyond. I could hear it bouncing off school lockers as we chased after it. I could tell the other students heard the racket too. Their laughter increased with every hit.

Once we exited the gym, we saw that it had finally stopped. I cringed when I saw our robot attacking Mr. Jacobs's floor buffer. Mr. Jacobs was the school custodian, and he held tight to the machine's handlebars as our robot pushed against it. Its plastic axes whacked at the buffer.

Noah slid to a stop and flicked the toggle switch at the back of the robot.

"Get to za chop ..."

"Sorry, Mr. Jacobs," Noah said.

"Yeah," Sam and I agreed. "Sorry about that."

Mr. Jacobs switched off the buffer and slowly removed the earbuds from his ears. He shook his head. "What are you kids up to now?"

There was a very good reason why he asked us that question. It was the same reason why I knew exactly how to operate that particular floor buffer he was using (as well many other pieces of custodial equipment). But you know what? That's a whole other story.

2

The Frequency Delinquency

THE SWIFT ACADEMY ISN'T THE BIGGEST SCHOOL,
so word of our robot's meltdown spread quickly. On
the way to history class I heard all kinds of bad Arnold
Schwarzenegger impressions repeating our robot's
catchphrase. At least Terry Stephenson was creative
with his altered Arnold phrase, "Get to za crappa!" His
group of friends laughed as I entered the classroom.
And honestly, I chuckled a bit too. That was a good one.

So, yeah, I wasn't so broken up about our robot's
utter defeat. Sure, it would've been great to have everything work perfectly. And our team had a major rebuild

ahead of us. But failing is not always a bad thing. My dad taught me from an early age that we fall down so we can learn to pick ourselves up again. And what teaches that better than science? Mistakes are ways to learn, overcome, and move forward. I would much rather have had our robot fail during a sparring match than during the final battle. This way, we can learn from our design mistakes and make it better than it was before.

"Hey, Tom," Amy said as she sat down at her desk next to mine. "Sorry about your robot."

"That's all right," I said. "We'll figure it out."

Amy shook her head. "I wish Sam was as calm as you. She barely spoke to me. She's busy making notes and sketching new designs."

"Noah was almost late for his next class," I told her. "He wanted to crack open the Choppa right then and there."

Yeah, Noah and Sam didn't have the same relaxed attitude as I did. Sure, I had written down my own notes and thoughts on what I believed caused the malfunction. But we really couldn't figure it out until we took the robot completely apart to find out what had gone wrong. There was no use in worrying about it if you couldn't do anything about it. The only thing I had to worry about now was Mr. Wilkins's history class.

I noticed that Amy had cleared her desk with the exception of a pen and a blank sheet of paper.

I pointed to Amy's desk. "What's going on?"

"Pop quiz," Amy replied.

I sighed. "*Of course* there's a pop quiz." I put away my textbook and dug out my own blank sheet of paper.

The Swift Academy faculty has been hopping on board an annoying trend lately—giving *way* too many pop quizzes. It's like they all held a meeting or something. You know what? They probably did. Maybe they're holding a contest among themselves to see who can give the most quizzes. We've been getting three or four pop quizzes a day, every day, in all classes.

Usually, the fact that the Swift Academy is different from other schools is a good thing. The teachers are always trying to mix things up in different ways. They just began changing class schedules midsemester. It's one of my favorite things so far. Take a break from algebra to learn geometry for a while? Sure! Put biology on hold and learn astronomy? Sign me up! I enjoy having interests over a wide range anyway. My father thinks I spread myself too thin sometimes. But if it's school sanctioned, what are you going to do?

However, I haven't run into *anyone* who enjoys the new pop-quiz trend. I've even had some fellow students ask me to talk to my dad about it. Hey, just because my name is on the school, doesn't mean I have any special pull. Plus, my father established the Swift Academy; he doesn't run it. He's too busy managing Swift Enterprises next door to police school curriculum.

To me, the worst part about the new pop-quiz trend was the distraction. It was hard enough having regular schoolwork and homework without the added stress of a test that may or may not happen. Besides, I had way more important things to worry about—like working on our killer robot!

"All right, sports fans," said Mr. Wilkins. That was his favorite nickname for his students. I don't know why; grown-ups are weird sometimes. "Let's have a little pop quiz on last night's reading assignment, shall we?"

There were moans as people put away their textbooks. Incidentally, Mr. Wilkins was one of the few teachers who insisted everyone have a physical textbook instead of the usual digital versions on students' school-assigned tablets.

I glanced around as Mr. Wilkins projected the test questions on the main board. Despite the scattered moans, many of the students were already set for the quiz. Was the pop-quiz trend so predictable that kids just assumed there would be one as soon as they got to class?

The quiz was about the Napoleonic Wars and wasn't too difficult. Luckily, I had retained most of what I'd read the night before. I know I didn't ace the quiz, but I'm sure I passed.

When the quiz was over, Mr. Wilkins cleared the screen and brought up a map of North America. "Please turn to page nighty-eight of your textbooks. Now, even though we in the United States see the War of 1812 as its own war, Europeans see it as more of a footnote in the Napoleonic Wars."

As I dug my book out of my backpack, something strange happened. Several high-pitched chirps sounded all around me. It was as if a bunch of phones received a text at once. A group of students must have timed an alert to go off.

Surely this was some kind of group prank for the teacher. I leaned back to watch the show.

"Many historians have speculated why Napoleon seemed to get the short end of the stick with the Louisiana Purchase," Mr. Wilkins continued. He didn't even skip a beat. Either Mr. Wilkins had an excellent poker face or he truly didn't notice the cacophony of tones.

Then it hit me. The chirps I heard must've been mosquito ringtones.

Speaking of trends, mosquito ringtones were a big deal with students a while back. It turns out that most adults over the age of thirty can't hear higher audio frequencies. Most of my friends made their text alerts what they call a "mosquito ringtone," so adults wouldn't hear when they'd received a text. Even I had one for a bit.

Little known fact: This audio discovery was originally made by a company in England. They created a speaker system that emitted an annoying high-pitched sound that kept kids from loitering in front of shops, but wouldn't bother the adult customers. But when mosquito ringtones came along, the kids got to turn the tables on the adults.

It was weird that everyone had received a text at the same time, though. I thought for sure it would've been a prank. That's when I noticed several students pulling out their phones. They each stealthily checked their screens before returning their phones to a pocket, purse, or backpack.

I turned to Amy to see if she had seen what I saw, but she was busy taking notes. The girl had a photographic memory, but she took taking notes very seriously. I didn't get it, but I wasn't going to bug her.

I scanned the class again and noticed several students had slipped out their tablets. I recognized pages from textbooks from other classes.

Deena Bittick sat in the row next to me, opposite Amy. She carefully hid her tablet behind her history textbook. She scanned through what looked like her algebra digital textbook.

I leaned across the aisle. "What's wrong?" I asked in a whisper. "Napoleon not exciting enough for you?"

Deena frowned at me. "I have a pop quiz next period," she whispered.

"Probably," I joked. "Anyone who's anyone is doing it."

"I *know* I am," Deena said. "Pop Chop told me."

Pop Chop? Who was she talking about? Several students had weird nicknames around the school. There was a Scooter, a Woody, and even a Stinky—Steve Krieger was never going to live down that failed chemistry experiment. But I had never heard of Pop Chop.

"I'm sorry. *Who* told you?" I asked.

"Not a *who*," Deena explained. "Pop Chop's an app."

I must've had a puzzled expression on my face because Deena sighed and slipped out her phone. She switched it on and pulled up a colorful loading screen. A cartoon hatchet sliced through a piece of paper with a red *F*- printed on it.

I reached for her phone. "Where did you . . ."

"Mr. Swift, do you have something to add?" asked Mr. Wilkins.

Startled, I jerked my hand back. I felt my face flush as everyone turned in my direction, and out of the corner of my eye, I saw Deena ease her phone back into her pocket with the sleight of hand of a skilled magician. If I weren't so embarrassed at the moment, I'd be downright impressed.

"Uh . . . ," I said, wringing my hands. "Napoleon wasn't actually short like everyone thinks." It was the first thing that popped into my head. "He was actually five feet, eight inches tall. Average height for that time period."

That was something I read on the Internet. I hoped it was right. Right or not, it got a laugh from the class.

"Close," Mr. Wilkins replied. "Five feet seven." He took the opportunity to remove his glasses and wipe one of the lenses on his shirt. "Oddly enough, the current lecture isn't about Napoleon's height." He replaced his glasses as chuckles rippled throughout the class. "It's about his role in the War of 1812. Anything to add about that?"

"No, sir," I replied. "Sorry."

"To continue," he said, turning to the projected map.

It took me a while to tune back in to the lecture and actually start taking notes. All I could think about was that weird app. Did one of the Swift Academy students create it? There were some brilliant programmers at our school, but I didn't think any of them had figured out a way to predict the future.

3

The Notification
Escalation

AS CLASS DISMISSED, I GATHERED MY THINGS
and caught up with Amy out in the hall. We hadn't seen
a lot of Amy lately. She spent all of her free time fencing. The team was having tryouts soon and she wanted
to get one of the limited spots.

"Nice Napoleon trivia," she said with a grin. "That
was from Lilo's Top Ten Historical Myths, wasn't it?"

"The first thing I thought of," I admitted, rolling
my eyes. No surprise that she had seen the same site
and had it memorized, of course. "But hey, before I got

busted, Deena was showing me this new app. It's called Pop Chop, I think?"

Amy smiled and was about to reply, but then froze. Her eyes cut up and to the left, as if remembering something. "Can you tell me about it later?" she asked. "I have to ask Mr. Jenkins a question before my next class."

"Sure," I replied. "Talk to you later."

I pulled out my phone as Amy disappeared into the flow of migrating students. As I made my way to the stairs, I pulled up the App Store and entered "Pop Chop" in the search field. The app came up right away and I read the summary as I climbed the stairs.

Are you tired of being caught off guard by pop quizzes? This crowdsourced app will subtly alert you if there is a pop quiz in your immediate future. Simply enter your school, class schedule, and alert schedule. Then let Pop Chop do the rest! But don't forget to log any pop quiz you encounter. Pop Chop only works if we all work together!

As I reached the second floor, I scrolled back to the top of the sales page, checking for the price. To my surprise, the app was free. I was curious to learn more, so my thumb instinctively shot to the Download button.

Then I paused. The app seemed kind of like cheating

to me. I didn't think I'd get in trouble for simply having the app installed on my phone, but something about it didn't seem right. Instead of downloading it, I switched off my phone and slid it back into my pocket.

When I got to the computer lab, Noah was already there. I grabbed my usual seat at the computer beside his.

"Are you getting all kinds of Arnold jokes?" he asked.

"Oh yeah," I replied. I told him about the "crappa" one. It was too good not to share.

Noah shook his head. "I don't care. I don't want to change the name. It still makes me laugh."

"We'll return the Choppa name to its former glory once we figure out what went wrong," I said. We hadn't had the chance to work on our robot since its embarrassing meltdown.

"I have some ideas about that," said Noah.

We tossed around some theories and possible ways to beef up the Choppa's defenses before the bell rang. Once it did, the rest of the students settled in front of their assigned computers and logged in. Mr. Varma rose from his desk.

"Okay, before we move on to our next exercise," our programming teacher began, "we're going to have a teensy little pop quiz on yesterday's material."

"Here we go again," I groaned.

I glanced around for solidarity, but only three or four students seemed upset about the pop quiz. Granted, Mr. Varma's melodic voice made almost any bad news sound cheery, but there should've been more grumblings from my fellow students. Were these quizzes so commonplace that everyone simply accepted the inevitable? Were they just a way of life now? My lips tightened as I shook my head. I didn't think it was right.

"Go to today's folder and open the file labeled PQ47," Mr. Varma instructed.

I put my feelings of injustice aside and did as he said. Thirty questions filled my screen. I was relieved when I saw there were only true-or-false questions. Sweet! Fifty-fifty shot.

Luckily, the test wasn't very hard and I'm pretty sure I more than passed it. I could tell I wasn't the only one who felt that way. It wasn't long before most of the students had finished.

"When you finish the quiz, go back to today's folder," Mr. Varma instructed. "Open today's exercise and begin programming. I'll be coming around to answer any questions and see how you're doing."

Mr. Varma's classes were usually pretty relaxed. He'd give us a programming problem to solve—create a timer or build a simple animation—and we'd use whichever programming language we were working on to solve that problem. With the tools we'd learned, everyone would come at the problem a little differently.

A steady stream of tapping came from Noah's nearby keyboard. My best friend was a programming machine. As usual, he'd have the problem solved in no time.

I was so focused on the assignment that I had completely forgotten about the Pop Chop app. That was, until the next alert came through.

Ding-ding. Ding-ding.

The same high-pitched tones erupted all around me. They seemed to come from everyone's phones at once. I glanced around and all the students seemed to ignore the sound—or at least pretended to ignore it. One by one, people began to secretively check their phones. Once again, the only adult in the room didn't seem to hear anything. Mr. Varma continued to move about the lab, offering assistance.

The chatter of Noah's keyboard silenced like a faucet being shut off. The abrupt stillness from his area caught my attention. He was good, but surely he couldn't be finished with the assignment already.

To my surprise, Noah had slipped his phone from his backpack and was checking the Pop Chop app.

"Dude," I whispered. "You too?"

Noah shrugged. "Me too what?"

"That app," I replied, pointing to his phone. "When did you start using that?"

"Isn't it cool?" asked Noah. His face lit as he spoke. "If you get surprised with a pop quiz, you log it in the app and it warns the next class of students that a quiz is coming."

"I know what it is," I said. "Don't you think that's cheating?"

"How?" asked Noah. "No one's passing along the answers. It's just a heads-up, you know? Almost everyone has it now. We're fighting back against all these crazy pop quizzes."

"If everyone has it, why haven't I heard about until now?" I asked.

Noah shook his head. "I don't know. Maybe people thought you'd report it to the teachers since . . . you know."

I frowned. "Because my name's on the school, right? You know me better than that."

Noah pointed to his chest. "Yeah, *I* know, sure. But hey, I'm in the same boat. Ronny Jenkins *just* told me about it last period. I'm probably the last to know too, because we're buds."

Suddenly this thing felt like a big conspiracy. Now it wasn't just the teachers being kept in the dark about this, but me, too. I thought I'd gotten past that sort of bias with most of my classmates. I had worked hard to prove that I was just another student with no special privileges. I never ran to my dad with a complaint about a teacher or a low test score. I never used my name as a strategy to get special assignments or first use with new supplies or lab equipment. I took my grades as they came and waited in line with everyone else.

"Who created this app, anyway?" I asked.

"I have no idea," Noah replied. "But I'm thinking it's someone in our school."

"Why's that?"

"Well, when you set up the app, it asks you to choose your school from a drop-down list," Noah explained. "Except the Swift Academy is the only school listed. It's like the app is set up for tons of others but ours is the only place it works for now."

"Maybe it's still in the testing phase," I suggested.

Noah shrugged. "I don't know, but it works for me. All these pop quizzes were starting to get to me."

I agreed with him there. A feeling of dread had been introduced into my school days since the pop-quiz trend had taken hold. The tests were so frequent that I usually felt like an ax was about to fall every time I stepped into a classroom. I'm sure the app creator saw it that way too. Maybe that's where the app got its logo.

Still, the whole thing made me feel uneasy.

4

The Restoration
Deliberation

"I'M NOT EVEN GOING TO TRY TO DIAGNOSE THIS
here," Noah said as he carefully unplugged the circuit
board. "I'll put in the backup board and work on the
damaged one at home."

"Sounds good to me," I said as I tested another relay.
"But either way, we have to figure out how to protect it
this time."

Noah had come over to my house after school and
had dinner with my father and me. After that, we hauled
the Choppa into the garage and took it apart on one of
my dad's big worktables.

Sam was supposed to join us but she had a last-minute family obligation. They were visiting her aunt in the hospital. It didn't sound like anything serious, but certainly more important than hanging out at a friend's house working on a robot.

Ding.

That didn't stop Sam from texting us any ideas she had. I put down the relay and picked up my phone.

"Another text from Sam," I said as I scrolled through her message. "She wonders if a foam piece around the board will help absorb some of the impact from attacks."

Noah nodded at the pile of foam sheets on the table. "I thought of that earlier. We'll have to test it, though. The heat from the circuitry may melt it."

My thumbs flew across the screen as I quickly wrote her back. I put my phone down and moved on to the next relay.

"You know, we have to protect it from attacks from the top as well as the sides," I said. "Some of those grippers are going to be vicious."

Just like the shows on television, Mrs. Scott's students had come up with a wide range of battling robots. There were flippers—robots with giant spatula-like devices made to flip other robots onto their backs. If a robot couldn't right itself, it would lose. There were also wedges, which were fast robots shaped like a ramp. They could speed under the competition and flip them from underneath.

We had to watch out for robots like ours—made for awesome destruction. Those, like Flailing Grade, struck their enemies with blunt objects like a flail or even a hammer. We were also concerned with the grippers and crushers. Those robots had powerful claws that could crush another robot's outer shell. It was best just to keep out of their reach.

Ping. It was Sam again.

I snatched up my phone and read her latest text. "She wonders if the circuits could be suspended somehow," I reported. "With something like little bungee cords."

Noah grabbed a handful of the micro bungee cords he had brought over. "You saw me bring these in, right? Already thought of it."

I read aloud as I texted Sam back. "Another good idea. Thanks."

"You keep telling her 'good idea'?" asked Noah. "I

thought of those things already. Now she's going to think she came up with everything."

"You *both* came up with those ideas," I said. "Just not at the same time."

"Yeah, but she doesn't know that," said Noah. "Now she's going to think that she came up with everything and I'm just the guy who drives the thing."

I pointed at the robot. "Hey, do you want me to help with this? Or would you rather I sit here all night typing out stuff like 'That's a good idea, Sam, but Noah already thought of it and even brought along a handful of mini bungee cords'?"

Noah put his hands on his hips. "Maybe I would."

Ping.

I sighed and pulled up her new text. "She also suggests some kind of crumple zone," I reported. "Like they have in cars. Whatever material that will fold and absorb impact."

Noah stared at me, mouth agape. "Okay, that's a really good idea," he finally admitted. "I didn't think of that one."

I pointed at my phone and raised my eyebrows. "Want me to tell her it's a good idea? Because I can tell her you already thought of that one, too."

Noah pointed a screwdriver at my phone. "Just text her back already."

I read aloud as I typed once again. "'Noah says best idea yet. Exclamation point. Exclamation point. Smiley face emoji.'"

Noah rolled his eyes as he went back to work on the new circuit board.

Ping.

"They're at the hospital," I reported. "She's done texting for the night."

We worked in silence for a while, Noah reinforcing all the connections to the backup circuit board while I finished checking the relays. I only had to replace one.

"So, did you get it?" Noah asked.

"Get what?" I asked back.

"You know? The app," he said.

I sighed. "No. It sounds cool and all. But it just doesn't seem right."

"I know you think that now," Noah said, pointing at me with a screwdriver. "But when you *try* it . . ."

Noah didn't finish. The entry door opened and my father stepped inside the garage. He had changed out of his suit and tie and now wore sweats. Judging from the towel over his shoulder and the sweat on his brow, he had just finished his evening workout. "How's it going, fellas?"

"We're getting there," I replied.

Over dinner, Noah and I had recounted our robot's losing bout. He knew we had a lot of work to do to get the Choppa up and running again. Now, we caught him up on Sam's (and Noah's) thoughts about how to insulate the inner workings of our robot from heavy attacks.

"Maybe you can use a little of all three systems," my dad suggested. "Build in a fail-safe in case one of them doesn't work."

"That's a good idea," I said.

"Mr. Swift, I have a question for you," said Noah.

"Shoot," my dad said.

"You know about all those pop quizzes we've been having lately?" Noah asked.

I caught my breath. What was he doing? After all that talk today about people not telling me about the app because of my dad? Now my best friend was going to make it look like I ratted out the entire school.

My dad laughed. "Tom has complained about them

almost every night. Cutting into his robot time, I hear."

"Well, hypothetically speaking," Noah continued, "what if I'm in a class and I get a pop quiz?" He pointed at me. "And then Tom has the same class, but next period. Would it be wrong for me to warn him about that quiz?"

My dad raised an eyebrow. "Do you give him the hypothetical *answers* to this hypothetical quiz?"

Noah shook his head. "No, nothing like that. I just let him know that one's coming up." He spun the screwdriver through his fingers and glanced at me. "Now, is that cheating?"

"Well, it is called a *pop* quiz for a reason," my dad said.

I smiled and nodded ever so slightly at my friend.

"But then again," my father continued, cocking his head, "your teachers know that you all talk to each other. They can't seriously expect you to keep this information to yourselves. So as long as you're not giving away the questions or answers, then I don't think it's cheating."

Noah nodded and smiled smugly.

"Ah, but what if he *texted* me the warning?" I asked.

"What's the difference these days?" My dad smirked. "The way you kids text all the time, I'm surprised you're not texting me your questions right now."

That night, after we drove Noah home, I went straight to my room. I did what I've done every night since the pop-quiz craze began. I got ready for bed and then hopped into my gyro-chair for some extra studying. The chair was a working prototype I'd built involving a chair suspended from the ceiling with bungee cords (the full-size ones) and a crude gyroscope. In theory, I could shift to any position in the chair and it would remain level. I thought my design showed a lot of promise. I had only fallen out of it twice so far.

I turned on my tablet and scanned a bit of material from each of my classes. I had to be ready for any pop quiz that came up tomorrow. It really seemed unfair— we had to do our usual homework load *and* study for a test that may or may not happen?

I put my tablet down and rubbed my eyes. I sighed, pulled out my phone, and downloaded the app.

5

The Ethical Assessment

"NO WAY!" I HEARD NOAH SAY AS I ENTERED algebra class the next morning. He was turned around, talking to Amy. When he saw me enter, he waved me over. "Hey, Tom. You gotta hear this."

"Hear what?" I asked as I plopped into my desk beside Noah's.

"Guess who's giving Amy fencing lessons?" he asked.

I looked at Amy. "Who?"

Amy wrung her hands together. "Michel Villa," she said quietly.

"The best fencer on the team?" I asked. "Wait. Isn't

he the one you're scheduled to fence first during try-outs?"

Amy nodded.

Michel was a French exchange student and had taken the fencing team to a whole new level when he transferred over. He was tall, wiry, and had a massive reach. It was like the academy got a ringer. Part of the reason we saw so little of Amy lately is because she didn't want to lose too badly during her first bout.

"I don't know if that's really smart or . . ." I glanced at Noah and shrugged. "A bad strategic move?"

"Yeah," Noah agreed. "He's gonna figure out all your weaknesses."

Amy rolled her eyes. "There's no way I was going to beat him anyway. It's not like in a championship. I don't have to win to move on to the next opponent. I just have to win more bouts than I lose, and the team is selected from fencers showing the most promise."

Noah shrugged. "I guess it's fine if you're getting something out of it, then. At least Michel doesn't seem too bad. He was nice enough when I helped debug his program a few weeks ago."

"I think it's extremely smart," Sam interjected. She

shrugged off her backpack and sat at the desk beside Amy. "She's going to learn all *his* tricks so she can win that first match."

Amy laughed and shook her head. "It's not like that. Michel saw how hard some of us were working and offered to help. That's it."

"Making the team is pretty important to you, huh?" I asked.

Amy beamed. "Oh yeah. I love the precision and discipline of it all."

"That's you, all right," Sam said.

"But I also love the anonymity," Amy continued. "Behind the mask, no one can see if I'm cringing, frightened . . ."

"Or grinning like a crazy girl because you're having so much fun?" asked Noah.

"Yes!" Amy burst into laughter.

We laughed with her, and when she snorted, we all chuckled harder. Embarrassed, Amy hid her face with both hands. But her shoulders kept bobbing up and down as she continued to laugh behind her mask.

The first bell rang and we all settled down. Mr. Jenkins brought up five problems on the screen for . . .

you guessed it. A pop quiz. I sighed and dug out a pencil and paper along with the rest of the class. This was getting ridiculous. Any doubts I had about downloading the app the night before were blown away.

The test wasn't too bad and took only about fifteen minutes for everyone to complete. And that was another thing—that's fifteen minutes of teaching time gone, right there. Why were the teachers wasting valuable time *and* needlessly stressing out their students?

As Mr. Jenkins finally began the morning lecture, I noticed several students slipping out their phones. They opened the Pop Chop app and logged the algebra quiz. First period classes didn't get any notice from the app, but the rest of the classes would now be forewarned.

I was going to log the quiz myself but with so many others doing it, it would be flagged for the other classes anyway. I even saw Noah sneak his phone out and report the quiz.

"So Noah has that stupid app too?" Sam whispered in my ear. "Does everyone have that thing now?"

I leaned back in my desk and angled my head. "We just found out about it yesterday," I whispered. "I only downloaded it last night."

She gave my shoulder a shove. "Tom Swift. I can't believe you."

"Hey, I'm sick of these tests just like everyone else," I said. "Don't you have it?"

"No," Sam shot back. "It's cheating."

I shook my head. "No, it's not. Nobody's passing along the answers. It's just, like, you know, an early warning system."

It was weird. Now I felt like Noah when he was trying to convince me. Somehow, I didn't think I was doing as good a job. I guess not all of my doubts were blown away after all.

"So you don't have it," I whispered. "Does Amy have it?"

"Why would she have it?" Sam asked. "She has a photographic memory."

I nodded. "Good point." I glanced back at Amy, who eyed us nervously. Knowing her, she was probably worried we were going to get busted for talking in class.

"Does your father know about . . . ," Sam began, before Mr. Jenkins paused and turned in our direction.

I don't know about Sam, but I started taking notes like nothing had happened. Sam must've done the same thing behind me, because Mr. Jenkins just stared at us briefly before returning to his lecture.

We didn't try talking any more. Mr. Jenkins usually gave out just one warning glare before calling out students in front of the entire class.

I only heard Sam say one more word that period.

About halfway through the class, everyone's Pop Chop alarms went off. And it sounded as if almost the entire class had the app installed now.

That's when Sam said, "Unbelievable," under her breath.

I glanced back and saw Sam shaking her head. Beside her, Amy's eyes were on Sam. Amy caught my gaze before returning her attention back to her notes.

I sighed and went back to my own notes. I didn't understand why Sam was so annoyed. No one was making her download the app.

I didn't bother sneaking out my phone and checking the app. The alert was bound to be for my next subject: chemistry. I already had my tablet out for my digital algebra textbook. After a few taps, my chemistry textbook came up too. I scrolled through the chapters to find the material we had covered the day before. For once a pop quiz wasn't going to take me by surprise.

After the bell rang, the subject of the Pop Chop didn't come up again between any of us. Sam, Noah, and I mainly talked about the next steps in prepping our robot. Amy was already headed to her next class.

I went upstairs to my chemistry class with newfound confidence. Even though I didn't know exactly what the test was about, it wouldn't take me by surprise. Besides, Mrs. Gaines never really seemed to take the pop-quiz trend so seriously. Her quizzes had been simpler than everyone else's.

Today was no different. All we had to do was list five ways to test a compound for traces of nickel. Since I had just reviewed that material, I aced the quiz with ease. I could've listed seven.

I turned in my test and leaned back in my desk triumphantly.

Tom Swift: one.

The System: zero.

6

The Causation Revelation

FOR THE NEXT FEW DAYS EVERYTHING WENT great. Gone were the days of my heart sinking whenever a quiz was announced. Outside of first period, I was ready for every pop quiz they threw at me. My mood improved incredibly and I had more confidence strolling into every classroom.

It wasn't just my spirits that were lifted. All the academy students seemed to be more cheerful. It was as if we were a species that had overcome a drastic environmental change. Our habitat had been flooded, so we developed gills to survive.

Unfortunately, it wasn't just the students who adapted. That's right, it didn't take long for the faculty to discover the app. No one came out and banned the app, but they did try to find ways to make it useless. Some teachers varied their quiz schedules to every other class. Some changed it to every other day. They tried their best to put the *pop* back in pop quiz.

But it didn't matter. The genius of the app meant that as long as teachers quizzed more than one class, most kids still knew when the tests were coming.

Sam was still against the app, but at least she had stopped giving Noah and me grief about it. We were too busy fine-tuning and upgrading the Choppa. The big robot battle was only a week away.

BAM!

Back in the gym, we watched Crab-a-saurus crash into the back of Flatliner. Crab-a-saurus had two large pincers that could theoretically crush the outer shell of any robot it caught. Of course, since this was just another sparring match, its claws were only set to half power.

Flatliner didn't need any restrictions. It was a wedge robot designed to flip its enemies by sliding under them.

It was built for speed. And it would need all of that speed to keep out of Crab-a-saurus's iron grip.

"Do you think we'll get to spar again before the final match?" asked Sam.

"I hope so," said Noah. He raised both hands. "The Choppa hungers for vengeance."

"I doubt it," I said. "There are still a few teams that haven't had a turn yet."

"That's too bad," said Amy. "But I'm sure you'll be great in the final battle."

This was about the only time we got to hang out with Amy. Now that she had a fencing tutor, even more of her free time was spent training for the tryouts. The only time when the four of us got to really catch up was when our robotics class and her gym class overlapped. We continued to share the gym—our robots sparring on one end and her class sparring on the other.

FWAM!

Flatliner slid under Crab-a-saurus and flipped it over. The robot flailed as it tried to right itself with both of its claws.

"*If* we face Crab-a-saurus and *if* we keep away from the claws and *if* we flip it over . . . ," Sam said. "We should move in quick and attack its underbelly." She pointed at the robot's exposed wheels. "There's hardly any shielding there."

Crab-a-saurus quickly flipped itself back onto its wheels.

"*If* we're quick enough," I added.

Amy pointed to the gym entrance. "What's that about?"

We turned and saw our principal, Mr. Davenport, and a brown-haired woman enter the gym. She wore a navy blue skirt and matching jacket. A man holding a large camera followed them.

"Hey, that's Olivia Garza from Channel 4 News," Sam said. "She interviewed me for my water project. What's she doing here?"

Sam had gotten a full scholarship to the academy (and lots of press coverage) after she invented a water-sourcing device. It's currently being tested to help drought-ridden areas across the globe.

"Don't worry, Sam," said Noah. "Water Girl is yesterday's news. I bet she's here to cover the robot battle."

Sam glared at Noah, but graciously didn't slap him for using a nickname she detested. She didn't have to. He did it himself when he slapped his forehead with one hand.

"Aw, man. The Choppa isn't even here," he said. "Why did she pick today to come?"

"Would you rather she had been here during our one and only sparring match?" I asked.

Noah cringed. "Oh, yeah. Bad enough that the entire school knows about our meltdown."

"It could be the entire city," Amy added.

We watched as the woman and her cameraman walked closer.

Noah patted down his hair. "Do I look all right?"

None of us answered. Instead, we watched as Olivia Garza veered away and headed for the other end of the gym.

"No way," said Noah.

"She's covering the fencing team," said Sam.

Noah shook his head and jutted a thumb over his shoulder. "When there are two perfectly good robots over there beating the crap out of each other."

"You better get back over there," Sam told Amy. "You could be famous."

Amy shook her head. "Uh-uh." She backed away. "No thank you."

Amy had always been extremely shy. Heck, we're

lucky she talks to *us*. There was no way she was going to be on camera.

"What if they want to show the entire class?" asked Noah.

Amy's breathing quickened and here eyes darted around as if looking for an escape route. We'd seen this before. She was headed for a full-blown panic attack.

"Here," I said presently, reaching for her mask. I snatched it out from under her arm and gently placed it over her head. I could no longer see her face behind the thick wire mesh.

Amy's shoulder's relaxed and her breathing slowed. "Thanks," she said. She took one more deep breath and exhaled. Then she trudged toward the other side of the gym.

We watched as the reporter interviewed a couple of the students. Amy kept her mask on but stayed behind the other students. After the cameraman lowered the camera, Amy jogged back toward us. She pulled off her mask.

"They're not interviewing the fencing team," she reported.

"But we just saw . . . ," Noah began.

Amy shook her head. "Yes, they interviewed some of the team members, but it wasn't about fencing."

"Then what was it about?" I asked.

"Let's get you over here, Mr. Davenport," said a woman's voice. It was Olivia Garza. They had moved closer to us, positioning our principal so both the practicing fencers and the robot battle would be behind him. Mr. Davenport removed his glasses and smoothed down the few remaining hairs he had on his bald head. After a moment, the cameraman raised the camera to his shoulder while the reporter stood beside the principal.

"Mr. Davenport," said the reporter. "What is *your* opinion of this Pop Chop app?" She held out the microphone to our principal.

My friends and I exchanged surprised looks.

"Well, in a school like the Swift Academy," Mr. Davenport began, "we're always seeing students invent creative ways to address the challenges we give them."

"Do you consider this app a way of cheating?" asked the reporter.

Davenport shook his head. "Some of our teachers may disagree, but I don't think it's cheating at all. In fact, I think it's a very clever study aid."

"Do you know who created the app in the first place?" she asked.

"Not yet," Davenport replied. "But if your investigation finds out, please let me know."

"Thank you, sir," said the reporter. She turned to the cameraman and ran her index finger across her throat.

"Danny, let's interview some of the teachers now," she told the cameraman.

Mr. Davenport gestured to the exit. "Right this way." He replaced his glasses and led them out of the gym.

"They're doing a whole story on Pop Chop?" I asked. "Cool! You know they'll uncover who created it."

"I'm sure they will," Sam added. "Ms. Garza is very thorough."

"I hope they do," Noah said, nodding his head. "I'd like to shake his or her hand." Noah pointed at Sam. "See? Even Davenport doesn't think it's cheating."

"Uh, guys?" Amy squeaked.

"What? You don't think a grown-up can be wrong?" Sam asked Noah.

"Maybe Mr. Davenport was just pretending to be okay with it," I suggested. "Maybe he's letting Channel Four News smoke out the creator."

"Guys?" Amy repeated, a little louder.

Sam's eyes lit. "That sounds about right. I bet it's all just an act."

Noah waved her off. "You gotta be kidding me."

"Guys!" Amy shouted.

The three of us stopped talking and turned to her. Amy looked down and fidgeted with her fencing mask.

"I did it," Amy whispered.

"You did what?" asked Sam.

Amy looked up and cringed. "I . . . I created Pop Chop."

7

The Invention
Dissension

"NO WAY!" A GRIN STRETCHED ACROSS NOAH'S face. "Way to go, Amy!" He reached out a fist and she tentatively bumped it with her own.

I was both surprised and impressed at the same time. Of all the people to create the controversial app, Amy would be the *last* person I would've guessed. Not only does she hate being the center of attention, but she is also a big stickler for the rules. Something like this would be way too much of a gray zone for her.

"And cool logo, by the way," said Noah.

Amy exhaled and grinned. "Thanks! Honestly, that

took almost as much time as it did to program the app. I got the idea from your robot, by the way. I hope you don't mind."

"Mind?" Noah put a hand to his chest. "I'm honored."

"Oh yeah," I agreed.

"I can't believe you!" Sam blurted.

The three of us were frozen by Sam's outburst. Amy lowered her head and fidgeted with her mask again.

Sam shook her head. "Why in the world would you build an app like that?"

Amy glanced up. "I . . . needed it." She gave a half smile.

"You?!" all three of us said simultaneously.

This was too much. Amy Hsu? Our Amy? *Needing* an app like that?

"You have a photographic memory," I said. "Quizzes have to be supereasy for you."

Amy shook her head. "You'd be surprised."

"What? You have to cram last-minute like everyone else?" asked Noah.

"No," Amy replied. "But I . . . I choke under pressure." She let out a long breath. "If I know there's going to be a test, that's one thing. But when it's a surprise, I just go blank." She turned her mask over in her hands. "My grades were slipping, and if they slip too low, I won't be allowed on the fencing team, no matter how much I practice."

"Whoa," said Noah. "I had no idea."

"I just needed something to take the pressure off," she explained. "Just a little warning, you know?"

I shook my head. "But why didn't you tell us about it?"

Amy shrugged. "I was going to right away. Honest. But after you started debating whether it was right or wrong . . . I chickened out."

Sam crossed her arms. "That's because, deep down, you know it's wrong."

"How is it wrong?" asked Noah. "You just heard the principal. Even he didn't think it was wrong."

"That's his opinion," said Sam.

"So, it's just *your* opinion that it's wrong," Amy countered. Her face began to flush. "No one is forcing you to use it."

"That's good, because I'm not," Sam said, her eyes narrowing in that dangerous way.

Things were heating up fast. Amy and Sam had been best friends since they came to this school. It was uncomfortable seeing them at odds like this.

I stepped between them. "I think the bigger issue right now is that news crew."

"What do you mean?" Amy asked.

"You heard what they said. They'll probably keep digging until they find out who's behind the app," I explained.

Sam pointed at Amy. "And when they find out it's you, they're going straight to Davenport. *Then* you'll find out if he really thinks your app is harmless or not."

"But it is," Amy pleaded. "It doesn't even give out the test questions or answers or anything."

"I agree," I said. "But maybe it would be best to go to him before they do."

"Or remove the app altogether," Sam suggested.

"Don't do it, Amy," Noah warned. "That thing means way too much to so many people now."

Noah was right. Like it or not, this app was now bigger than one student trying to take the *pop* out of pop quizzes. This app was a morale boost for the entire school—well, maybe not the teachers.

"I . . . I don't know what to do," said Amy.

"That's called having a conscience, Amy," Sam

snapped. "Maybe you haven't memorized that page of the dictionary yet."

Amy gasped and stared at Sam with her mouth agape. Tears formed in her eyes before she turned and ran away.

8

The Persuasion Equation

AMY AND SAM DIDN'T TALK TO EACH OTHER THE rest of the day. Sam barely even spoke to Noah and me. Amy was still fencing in every free moment, so we didn't see much of her. The times I did see Amy and Sam together, they didn't even look in each other's direction.

"Everything all right, buddy?" my dad asked at dinner. "Pop quizzes getting you down again?"

"No," I replied. "I mean, yeah. They're still a pain and all, but I got it covered."

"Well something's eating you," he said.

I guess having my friends fighting affected me more

than I thought. Or, more likely, my dad could read me like a book—as always.

"Sam and Amy aren't talking to each other," I replied, mindlessly stirring my mashed potatoes.

I didn't want to go into detail about the argument because that would mean that I'd have to tell my dad about the app and who created it. I knew he would understand, and we've always been open and honest with each other. But I was already the last to find out about the app's existence because people were afraid I might report everything to my dad. I didn't want to be "that guy." The last thing I wanted was to prove anyone right, that I wasn't just a regular student. But still, I didn't like keeping things from my dad. It was an irritating balancing act that I was all too used to.

Luckily, he didn't press for details.

"That does happen sometimes," he said between bites. "We're all different and can't agree on everything." He dabbed the corner of his mouth with a napkin and nodded. "You know, it's been my experience that true friends can work past their issues. They realize their differences complement each other."

That was my dad, always with the words of wisdom.

And he was right. The four of us in our close-knit group *were* very different from one another. And we often complemented one another's strengths and weaknesses. That was also why we made such great teammates or lab partners.

I shook my head. "Thanks, Dad."

"For what?" he asked, raising an eyebrow.

"For telling me it will all work out," I replied. "Without actually saying 'It'll all work out.'"

He took another bite and smiled. "Oh, is that what I did?"

After dinner, I disappeared into my room to do homework. Since my mom died, my dad has always gone above and beyond to be there for me. Luckily, it wasn't in a smothering/helicopter parent sort of way. Both of us respected each other's need for quiet alone time.

Getting through my homework was more difficult than usual; I was still distracted by Sam and Amy's argument. It was like a puzzle or a math problem that my brain just wouldn't let go. Amy had clearly explained why she had created the app, but I didn't get why Sam was so opposed to it. She's always had a live-and-let-live attitude. Like Amy had said, no one was forcing Sam to use it. Why did it bother her that others did?

After I finished my homework, I decided to ask Sam myself. I pulled up my video chat program and sent her a chat request. She didn't answer. I tried again. Nothing. Either she was away from her computer or she was purposely ignoring my calls. I took a gamble on the second option. I grabbed my phone and shot her a quick text.

Come on, I typed.

I sent another video chat request. This time she accepted.

Sam's face appeared in a small box on my computer screen. "What is it?" she asked.

"Hi—uh," I stammered. "I just wanted to . . . see how you're doing."

Sam sighed. "I'm fine. I'll see you at school, Tom." She reached for her computer keyboard to end the chat.

"Whoa, hold up," I said.

Sam froze. "What?!"

"What are you mad at me for?" I asked.

Sam's shoulders slumped. "I'm not."

"Want to talk about it?"

"No," Sam replied. She massaged her temple. "Maybe. I don't know."

"Why are you letting this app get to you so much?" I asked. "Just think of it as a tool. Like a calculator or a ruler."

"Yeah, Tom," she said. "But you're usually not allowed to use a calculator during a test either."

I held up a finger. "But . . . sometimes you are," I countered. "And the teachers all know about the app now. None of them have banned it."

"That's true," she agreed.

I told her about Noah's hypothetical situation where someone tells a friend about an upcoming pop quiz.

"I guess that doesn't seem wrong," she said.

"What if that person sends a mass text to all of his or her friends?" I added.

Sam raised an eyebrow. "That feels like pushing it, to me."

"Why?" I asked. "Because of the amount of people they're telling?"

"Maybe," she said. "Or the use of technology."

"Okay, how about this?" I leaned closer. "What if I were to tape a sign outside the classroom that warns everyone about the test? It's low-tech *and* . . . I'm still telling a lot of people at once."

Sam's eyes lit. "Ah! But the teacher can find the note and decide to take it down. If you send a mass text, then he or she has no say in the matter."

She made a good point. And debating with Sam was always fun. Of course, it was usually about more interesting topics like the existence of aliens or time travelers visiting us from the future and the science (or lack) thereof.

"Sam. Seriously. Why does this bother you so much?" I asked. "You've been okay with bending the rules before."

It was true. Sam had a crafty side that was a little freaky sometimes. Her sneakiness had been invaluable when we helped find that hacker trying to penetrate my dad's computer system.

"Not when it comes to schoolwork, I don't," she corrected. "Or when it's self-serving."

"I didn't mean . . . ," I began.

"Look, you know how I got to this school. A great invention that could help 'save the world.'" She said the last part making air quotes. "Well, that's a lot of pressure,

65

you know? Sometimes I feel that everything I do here is being judged. *What will she come up with next? Was her one and only invention just a fluke?*" She shook her head. "This school is hard enough as it is. I don't want people to think that I have to cheat to stay here."

"Sam, you're one of the smartest people I know," I said.

"That's nice of you to say and all," she said. "But that only adds to the pressure, you know."

"Okay, I get why *you* don't use the app," I said. "But why do you care if anyone else does?"

Sam rubbed her eyes. "Maybe I'm a little jealous, okay? I know these are my self-imposed standards. But maybe I'd like a little early warning for all these stupid quizzes. But I . . . I just can't."

"And that's why you're mad at Amy?" I asked. "For building the app?"

"Well, yeah," she said, then cringed. "I mean . . . no. Not really."

"Then why?"

Sam stared down for a while and then sighed. "I guess I was mad because . . . well, she didn't tell me that she was the one who created it. I mean . . . this app is all that anyone is talking about and she doesn't say a word to me? I'm supposed to be her best friend."

"You're right," I said. "We've all been talking about this app. And you've been very . . . open about your opinion. Don't you think that's why she didn't tell you? You don't want to be judged for using the app. She didn't want to be judged by her best friend for creating it."

Sam opened her mouth to reply but stopped. She raised an eyebrow instead. "All right, Swift. You snuck up on me with that one." She let out a long breath and ran a hand through her short brown hair. "I was probably way too hard on her."

"Hey, whether you believe in it or not," I said, "or whether you want to use it or not, you have to admit it's an ingenious app."

Sam smiled. "She never gives herself enough credit."

I nodded. "That makes two of you."

"Do you think she took me seriously and deleted the app after all?" Sam asked.

I shook my head. "I don't know. She was pretty upset."

"I'll talk to her tomorrow," Sam said. "Thanks."

I raised my hands. "That's what friends are for."

After we logged off, I stood and grabbed my phone.

I felt pretty good helping two friends get back together. But I also felt more confused than ever about the app. Here I was defending it and now Sam had planted seeds of doubt back into my mind. I turned the phone over in my hand as I heard a knock on my door.

My father stood in the open doorway. "I just watched the news and they ran the most interesting story about the academy."

I plopped back in my chair. I had completely forgotten about the news crew.

"So you know about the app, huh?" I asked.

"Pop Chop?" my dad asked. "I take it this has something to do with the hypothetical questions Noah asked me the other day."

I nodded. "Yeah. What do you think?"

"Mr. Davenport seems okay with it," my dad replied. "It sounds as if he's not banning the use of it."

"No, he hasn't," I said. "But that's not what I mean. Do you think it's cheating?"

My dad shrugged. "It doesn't matter what I think."

I laughed. "Of course it matters what you think. That's why I asked."

My father shook his head. "It doesn't matter what I

think because I'm not using the app." He pointed at me. "It only matters what you think."

I shook my head and sighed. My dad was frustrating like that sometimes. Once again, he didn't just come out and say it. But he didn't have to. I guess if it felt as if you were doing the wrong thing, you probably were.

"You're probably right," I said.

Even though it wasn't against the rules, using the app did feel a little like cheating. I could keep using it and always have that twinge of guilt, or I could get rid of it and have a clean conscience about the whole thing. I decided to go ahead and delete the app from my phone. My dad turned to leave just as I turned my phone on.

Ding-ding.

The Pop Chop update alert went off.

"By the way—" My dad stopped but didn't turn around. "Did you know that some adults can still hear a mosquito ringtone?"

My jaw dropped.

My dad raised a finger. "Little-known fact." He disappeared down the hallway.

I laughed as I scrolled through my phone. Sure

enough, the Pop Chop app indicated that an update was available. I almost ignored it and deleted the app as planned.

But if an app developer wanted to delete an app from everyone's phone, he or she would have to issue an update that would do just that. Otherwise, it would be up to the individual user to delete it.

I went through with the update to see if that's what Amy was doing. Even though I had already made the decision to get rid of the app, I felt better knowing I wouldn't be the only one.

After the update went through, the app launched. The update didn't delete the app after all. Instead, the settings screen came up and the "Enter School" option appeared.

That was weird. I had already selected my school. Well, "selected" would be overstating it. The only option available before was Swift Academy.

That had changed.

When I tapped the drop-down menu, a huge list of schools appeared. I recognized some of the names, but most of them were unfamiliar. It took a lot of scrolling to get down to the "S" section to select the academy.

After I made the selection, another screen appeared. This one was completely new. "New Feature" was printed at the top with a short paragraph below.

Now available: Use your camera to photograph a quiz and upload it to the Pop Chop database. Users will have the option to simply be alerted to the upcoming quiz and/or preview the quiz itself.

That wasn't the biggest surprise, though. When I swiped past that page, another one came up.

Trial Period Over, the page read. *To continue using Pop Chop, pay $4.99.*

I couldn't believe it. There was no doubt about the app now. There was no way the principal or any of the teachers would be okay with this. This was definitely cheating—for profit!

What was Amy thinking?

9

The Appropriation Vexation

THE CELL TOWERS WERE BURNING UP THE NEXT morning as Sam, Noah, and I exchanged texts about the latest update. We were all shocked that Amy would make such drastic changes to the app. Each of us also tried to text Amy several times. None of us got an answer.

My father agreed to drop me off at school early so I could meet up with my friends. I didn't want to tell him about the new development until I had more answers. This also meant that I couldn't tell him about my decision—that I had already decided to dump the app in the first place. Of course I wanted him to be proud of my choice, but now that was the last thing on my mind. I was too worried about my friend.

After my father dropped me off, I waited on the school's front steps. Sam showed up next, followed by Noah.

"Amy's mom said she dropped Amy off early," Sam reported. "So she's probably in the gym for fencing practice."

We ran up the steps and went inside.

"Man, I still can't believe Amy doubled down like that," Noah said.

"I think I pushed her too hard," Sam admitted. "Now when they uncover who's behind the app, she's really going to get in trouble."

"Yeah, it's full-blown cheating now," Noah added.

"Or at least the ability to," I said.

"Why would she add all those other schools?" asked Sam.

"Are you kidding?" Noah rubbed his thumb and index finger together. "That means big bucks after that news story last night."

"You think people will really pay for it?" asked Sam. "I can't believe the academy's students will go for it."

"First of all, there's no way Davenport will let this fly," said Noah. "I bet there's an announcement before lunch banning the app entirely." He shrugged. "But if he doesn't ban it ... then yeah, it's worth five bucks to keep the alerts coming."

Sam shook her head and pressed forward. "We have to talk her into taking it down."

When we reached the gym, there were only three fencers there. There was a tall, thin fencer sparring with a shorter one. The looming figure couldn't be mistaken for anyone other than Michel Villa. The fencer watching the bout had his mask off; it was Kyle Swan. The third one had to be Amy.

We strode across the gym floor as the sound of clashing foils echoed around us.

"Amy," Sam said. "We need to talk."

The fencers didn't stop.

"Yo, Ames!" Noah shouted as we approached.

"Halt!" Michel ordered. Both fencers lowered their foils and Michel removed his mask. He waved to Noah as we jogged over.

"Amy? She is not here this morning," Michel said in his French accent.

The shorter fencer removed his mask. It was Toby Nguyen.

"Have you seen her?" I asked.

"No, I have not," replied Michel.

"Okay, thanks," Noah said with a wave. "Sorry to bother you!"

"It's no bother," Michel said. He put his mask back on. "My program has been working great thanks to you. Happy to help, if I can."

We bid him farewell and headed straight for our first period class. She wasn't there either.

"You don't think she skipped school, do you?" I asked.

"Create a killer cheating app and ditch in one day?" Noah shook his head. "Not Amy."

We strolled around the nearly empty school, glancing in classrooms along the way.

Sam stopped and pulled out her phone. "I'm texting her again." Her thumbs flew across the screen.

To our surprise, we finally received a reply. A group text appeared on my screen. "In the library. Please help."

We jogged up to the second floor and ran down the hall to the library. We found Amy sitting at an empty table hunched over her laptop.

I exhaled with relief as I glanced around. We were completely alone. I guess my imagination went wild when I read her last text. I pictured her being held hostage or something.

Amy looked up as we approached. Her hair and clothes were disheveled and large bags hung under her eyes. Since Amy usually never had a hair out of place and her clothes were always meticulously pressed, it was like looking at another person entirely.

"What happened?" Sam asked.

"I've been up all night," Amy replied. "Someone took over my app and locked me out."

10
The Repercussion Discussion

WE ALL SAT AROUND THE TABLE WHILE AMY explained what happened. Noah had Amy's laptop, trying to log back into the App Store website.

"I hadn't changed the app's programming in a couple of days," Amy explained. "When the update alert happened last night, I thought it was a mistake." She rubbed her temple. "I tried to log in but my password wouldn't work."

Noah pointed to a page on the website. "It says here that you turned over the app to some company called Insider, Inc."

"That's what they told me," Amy said. "I was on the phone with Tech Support for a couple of hours. They said I gave away all rights and control over the app." She shook her head frantically. "But I didn't!"

"We believe you," I said.

Amy wrung her hands. "And when I saw what they did to my app . . ." She glanced up at Sam. "I know you think my app was cheating before, but now it's really cheating. And they're making money off it?"

Sam gave a half smile. "I'm sorry, Amy. I overreacted before."

Amy shook her head. "No, you were right." She covered her face with her hands. "This was so stupid. Stupid!"

I've never seen Amy so upset. Sure, we've witnessed the odd panic attack when she thought she might have to give some kind of presentation in front of a group of people. But this was more like utter devastation.

"Don't worry about that right now," I said, putting a hand on Amy's shoulder. "What did the phone company say? Can they clear everything up?"

Amy lowered her hands and sighed. "Well, after I spent tons of time proving to them that I was who I said

I was, they said they would conduct an investigation."

"So, that's good, right?" Sam asked. She attempted a brave smile. "If your account was hacked, they'll figure it out."

"Yeah, but their investigation could take weeks," Amy explained, her eyes welling up with tears.

I cringed. "Not so great."

Amy jutted a thumb at her computer. "In the meantime, someone has turned my app into a cheating tool. Everyone's going to think I did this."

For the moment, only the four of us knew that Amy created the app. Well, us and the person who hacked it. But if the news crew kept digging, they would more than likely find out who created it in the first place. Reporters always had various contacts in different companies. They might find someone who would leak confidential information. And all they would need was the name.

"Then we need to get ahead of this," I announced. "We go to Mr. Davenport and tell him the entire story."

"What?" asked Amy and Noah.

"Look," I said pointedly. "If you tell him now, before school starts and before anyone uploads quizzes, then that proves you're innocent. He'll ban the app and you'll have nothing to gain."

"Yeah," agreed Sam. "How can you make money if you know your app will be banned?"

Amy ran a hand through her hair. "Okay. You're right." She looked up at us with a half smile. "Will you all come with me?"

Sam grinned. "Of course!"

The four of us made our way down to the first floor. The halls began to fill as more students arrived for school. None of them seemed to notice how we shuffled along. I don't know about my friends, but it felt as if we were marching toward death row.

When we arrived at the front office, Ms. Lane, the office manager, was working at her computer.

"Is Mr. Daven . . . ?" Amy squeaked before clearing her throat. "Is Mr. Davenport in?"

"He's in his office, hon." Ms. Lane smiled. "You can go on back."

We filed past the front counter and headed toward the principal's office. Even though I was just there to back up my friend, it still felt as if I was in trouble.

Mr. Davenport looked up from his desk as we

entered. "You know I have an open-door policy, but"—he glanced at his watch—"you're about to be late for class."

"This is important, sir," I said.

"All right." He leaned forward. "How can I help?"

"I created the Pop Chop app," Amy blurted out, and then slammed her eyes shut.

"Whoa, what?" the principal asked, taken aback. "*You* did, Miss Hsu?"

Amy tightened her lips and nodded.

Mr. Davenport leaned back in his chair. "Well, this is a surprise." He pointed at the rest of us. "And you all helped, I assume?"

Amy's eyes widened. "Oh, no, sir. It was all me. They're just here for . . . moral support."

"All right, then, Miss Hsu. I certainly give you credit for your ingenuity," he said. "The ethical gray area not withstanding."

"Ethical gray area?" I asked.

"But in the interview you said it was a helpful study aid," said Noah.

"I did," our principal agreed. "But since that report aired last night, I've received several e-mails from concerned parents. Most of them think the app is indeed cheating."

"Because it's an app?" asked Sam. "But what if a student were to tape a sign outside of class that—"

"Maybe . . . now's not the time to have that debate," I said, gently interrupting Sam. A smile pulled at the corners of my mouth—Sam was using my argument to defend her best friend. I took a deep breath, getting serious. "Mr. Davenport, something's happened that you should know about."

With Amy taking the lead, we told him about the app's latest update. His eyes widened as the story progressed.

Mr. Davenport tilted his head back and stared at the ceiling. "So you're telling me that anyone can photograph a test and upload it to this app?"

We all nodded.

"You know that's definitely cheating, right?" he asked. "No gray area at all with that."

"Yes, but it's not Amy's fault," Sam explained. She told him about how someone took control of the app and locked Amy out.

"You don't know who it was?" asked Mr. Davenport.

"No, but we're going to find out," said Noah. "I'm thinking it's someone in this school."

"So you're accusing another student of what could be a serious crime," Mr. Davenport said. "But you don't know who it is. It could be some hacker overseas, for all we know. Meanwhile, Miss Hsu just confessed to creating the app in the first place."

"But don't worry, sir," I said. "We'll figure out who it is."

Mr. Davenport removed his glasses and rubbed the bridge of his nose. "Well, Miss Hsu. I appreciate you coming here and telling me all this." He replaced his glasses and sat straight at his desk. "But due to the serious nature of these events, I have no choice but to suspend you while we conduct an investigation."

"Suspend her?" asked Sam.

"It's standard procedure for this sort of thing." Mr. Davenport stood. "You three get to your first period class. Miss Hsu, go collect your things while we call your parents."

11

The Postponement Proposition

WE WALKED AMY BACK TO HER LOCKER. HER lower lip trembled and I could tell she was fighting back tears. Luckily, most of the students had already gone to class. The hallway was nearly empty.

"Don't worry, Amy," said Sam. "We'll find out who did this."

"Even better," Noah added, "I'll find a way to log on to your developer site and we'll delete the app completely."

"We've got your back, Amy," I said. "You'll be cleared in no time."

"Thanks," Amy said, giving a weak smile. "But you better get to class. You're all going to be tardy."

"Aw, we still have some . . . ," Noah began, before the bell rang.

Oh, yeah. Having a photographic memory is not Amy's only superpower. She has a near-perfect internal clock.

The four of us shared a small laugh before parting ways.

Sam, Noah, and I were almost to the outside of our first class when it hit me. Any minute now Mr. Davenport would make an announcement banning all use of the Pop Chop app. How would we find the person responsible if he did that?

"I'll meet you inside," I told my friends. "I have to do one more thing."

I jogged back toward the front office. Now, I've never used my name to get special privileges at school. I've worked too hard to keep people from treating me differently as it is. But if I did, I would certainly throw my name around to try to get Amy reinstated. And even if it did work, it would only work once. As soon as my father heard about it, I'd be grounded for a year.

Right then, however, I felt a little differently. Maybe my name would give me just a few more minutes of Mr. Davenport's time. I only needed a small favor from him.

I reached the front office and Ms. Lane had stepped away from her desk. I ran past it and entered Mr. Davenport's office.

"What do you need now, Mr. Swift?" Mr. Davenport asked. "I have to make an announcement banning this app once and for all."

"Yeah," I said. "Could you, kind of, *not* do that?"

Mr. Davenport glared at me over the rim of his glasses. "Excuse me?"

"Well, we want to catch whoever hacked Amy's app, right?" I asked. "I'm not sure how we're going to do that yet, but if the app goes away, so does the person who controls it. They'll just fade like nothing ever happened."

"So, you think you can flush them out somehow?" the principal asked.

"Maybe," I replied. "Hopefully."

Mr. Davenport shook his head. "I don't know. With this app out there, the way it is, the pop quizzes are going to be useless."

I chuckled. "It's not like they were doing any good

anyway." I nearly winced after I spoke. That just kind of slipped out.

"What do you mean they aren't doing any good?" Mr. Davenport asked. His eyes narrowed. "I came up with the pop quiz regimen myself."

"They were your idea?" I asked.

"Certainly," he replied. "I wanted to make sure all the academy students got the most out of their education."

My stomach knotted. I have never told a teacher that he or she was flat-out wrong before, especially not the school principal. But if Mr. Davenport believed the quizzes were helping his students, he was way off base. Someone had to give him a student's point of view. And unfortunately for me, I was the only one here with the perfect opening. I took a deep breath.

"Well, excuse me for saying this, sir," I said, "but what if I told you the opposite was happening?"

"What are you talking about?" he asked, his eyes narrowing again. "And be honest."

"Okay." I nervously rubbed the back of my neck. "First of all, one of the great things about the academy is that all the teachers are so different. With all the pop quizzes, they're slowly starting to teach the same way, just throwing information out there."

"Really?" asked the principal.

"And the same goes with the students," I added. "We're just trying to remember what's going to be on the next test." I put a hand on my chest. "I can't speak for everyone, but learning used to be fun. Lately it's been more memorization than anything else."

"So you think there shouldn't be any tests?" asked the principal. "Just grade everyone on the honor system?"

"No, sir," I replied. "I'm not saying that at all. I'm saying that there are just too many of them right now. It's way too much pressure."

Mr. Davenport raised his hands. "If you've learned the material anyway, there should hardly be any pressure."

"Let me put it to you this way, sir," I said, leaning closer. "A student with a photographic memory, who can ace any test you put in front of her, created an app to relieve the stress of those tests. What does that tell you?"

Mr. Davenport's lips tightened as he drummed his fingers on his desk. "Well, that's a lot to think about." He pointed to his computer monitor. "But Mr. Swift . . . Tom.

There's no way I can ignore this app now. I'm going to be flooded with e-mails from parents by tomorrow morning. I guarantee it."

"Just give us a couple of days, sir," I said. "Please."

Mr. Davenport clenched his jaw and slowly shook his head. It looked as if all of this was for nothing. I didn't get through to him.

Then he sighed. "You have twenty-four hours."

12

The Calibration
Calculation

I MADE IT BACK TO CLASS WITH JUST ENOUGH
time to catch—you guessed it—that morning's pop
quiz. When it was over Mr. Jenkins began the day's lecture. As quietly as I could, I told Sam and Noah about
my conversation with Mr. Davenport.

"Twenty-four hours isn't enough time," Noah
whispered.

"It has to be," I said. "In the meantime, we should keep
an eye out and see if anyone is acting differently."

"What, you think someone will be walking around

counting all the money they made from the updated app?" asked Sam.

"I don't know," I replied. "We have to look for something."

I honestly didn't think that far ahead. That was *my* superpower: Come up with half a plan and wing it from there.

"I'm going to research the company name that supposedly bought Amy's app," Sam whispered. "Maybe I can track the person that way."

"Good idea," I said.

"Tom, all my software is on my home computer," Noah said. "I can't work on breaking the password until I get home."

I knew that my friend was an excellent programmer and a budding hacker, but I had no idea what he was talking about.

"What do you do at night?" I asked him. "Hack into the White House servers?"

"Oh, yeah." Noah nodded. "Do you remember when all those Secret Service agents swarmed my house and hauled away my computer equipment?"

"What? No!" I replied.

"Right, because it didn't happen," Noah said. "I'm not stupid, Tom." He glanced around. "But I have some tools that might do the job."

Sam shushed us just as Mr. Jenkins paused to stare in our direction. The three of us stared back blankly, pretending to write down the last thing he said. Noah even looked over his shoulder, pretending to look for what Mr. Jenkins was staring at.

Our teacher gave an impatient sigh and went back to his lecture. We didn't risk talking the rest of the class.

When the bell rang we split up and went about our usual business. Each of us vowed to keep an eye out for the app thief. Sam was right, though; I didn't really know what I was looking for. Everyone looked . . . well, normal.

There were plenty more pop quizzes, of course. But true to his word, Mr. Davenport didn't make a general announcement banning the app. Mosquito ringtones rang out every hour. I guess people *will* pay five bucks to keep the alerts coming. Whoever controlled the app now must be thrilled with the new income stream. And I didn't see anyone walking around counting money, unfortunately.

Halfway through third period, I received a text from Noah. **Meet me in the computer lab now!**

I made an excuse to go to the restroom and headed over to the lab. I knew Mr. Varma had a free period then, so I wouldn't be interrupting his class. There would just be the odd student there working on a project.

I reached the second floor, and Sam was right ahead of me. Noah must've sent her the same text. We entered the lab to find Noah sitting in front of a computer near the back. As I suspected, there were only a couple of other students there.

Noah grinned. "Guess what? I'm in."

"In what?" asked Sam.

"I cracked the password," he replied. "I'm in the app's developer portal."

"No way," I said, eyes wide. "I thought all your software was at home."

Noah leaned back. "I did it old-school. You see, I got to thinking . . ."

"Who cares how you did it," Sam said, leaning closer to the screen. "Let's get in there and—"

I held up a hand. "No, no, let him have this."

Noah bowed his head. "Thank you, kind sir."

Sam rolled her eyes and plopped down in a nearby chair.

"I got to thinking how this person got Amy's password," Noah continued. "There was a chance that he or she must've seen her enter it at some point."

I pulled up another chair. "So?"

"So, he would have had to memorize Amy's password on the fly," Noah continued. "Now, when someone creates a new password, especially in a hurry, they usually use a birthday or something easy. But since we know nothing about the perp . . ."

"Noah, come on," Sam said impatiently.

Noah raised his hands. "Fine, fine. The new password is one digit off from Amy's."

"Just one digit off?" asked Sam. "That's it?"

"It's an old hacker trick," Noah explained. "It's easy to remember and change back so it could be blamed on a keystroke error if need be."

I extended a fist. "Way to go, man."

Noah returned the fist bump. "Thanks."

"So let's go in there and delete the app," she suggested. "You can create an update that makes it delete itself from everyone's phones, right?"

Noah reached for the keyboard. "Easy-peasy."

"Wait, hold up," I said upliftingly. "If we delete the app, that's just as bad as Mr. Davenport banning the app from the school."

"Worse, actually," Noah said with a smirk. "It means whoever did this won't cash in from any of those other schools that are now listed."

"But what I mean is we won't be able to find out who stole the app in the first place," I explained.

"You're right," Sam said. She pointed to the screen. "Is there any way to find out who it is on this site? Maybe they updated Amy's profile?"

"First thing I checked," said Noah. "There's just a generic email address in the contact info. There's a bank account number for all the fees." He shook his head. "But unless you know someone in law enforcement, there's no way to see who it belongs to."

"Should we send him or her an e-mail?" Sam asked. "Flush them out that way?"

"They may not respond," I said. "Or take days to respond. If it's even a real e-mail address."

Noah chuckled. "If I knew who this person was, I could write some code that could send an embarrassing photo to every person's phone. It would be easy. He or she would go crazy trying to shut the app down."

Sam and I looked at each other and smiled. "That's it," I said.

Noah shook his head. "Dude, I said *if* I knew who it was."

Sam pointed at the computer screen. "No, but you could rewrite the code to do something else, right? What if you took away the pay features? Made the app free again?"

Noah grinned. "That could drive them crazy. Bunch of cash flying right out the window!"

"Good one," I said. "But then the perp would know someone's onto them. Can't you just make the app crash or something?"

"Ooh," Sam said. "If the app doesn't work, there's still a bunch of cash flying out the window."

Noah's eyes lit. "And there's a chance people would delete the faulty app altogether."

"Oh, yeah." I grinned. "And if it were me, I'd be nuts trying to get it running again as quickly as possible."

"Sounds like a plan," said Noah. He pulled up the app source code and began scrolling down the screen. "I could bury a flaw deep in Amy's original code. I know her programming style. I could make it look like it was her mistake in the first place."

"The app thief would have to scan the code, line by line, to find the error," Sam said. "He or she would spend *way* too much time trying to find the problem."

"Instead of doing schoolwork," Noah added as he scrolled. "We could look for someone ditching class, sneaking into the computer lab or the library."

I glanced around the computer lab. "But it can't crash now," I said. "We can't see anyone panicking if we're stuck in class."

Noah typed on the keyboard. "Leave everything to me."

13

The Surveillance Stratagem

THE THREE OF US MET UP AT LUNCH AND GOT IN line as early as possible. If everything went as planned then we wouldn't have much time to eat. We grabbed a table near the back and sat facing the rest of the room.

Noah pulled out his phone between bites. He set it on the table and checked the screen. "One minute to go."

My best friend and hacker extraordinaire had added a flaw into Amy's code easily enough. The tricky part was making it go into effect at the right moment. Luckily, the app developer site had a feature that let users schedule automatic updates. The site kept a record of the updates, of course, but not of *when* the updates were originally scheduled. If all went well, the app thief would think this was just an update Amy had scheduled earlier.

Noah had set it to update during lunch when *most* of the students would be in one place. We had a backup plan if no one freaked out in the cafeteria. We would just have to do things the hard way—check the school, room by room. Luckily, the Swift Academy wasn't huge, hence only one lunch period. It would take some running, but we could each take a floor and account for any stray student who wasn't in the cafeteria.

Noah checked his phone again. "Here we go," he said. "In three, two, one . . ."

Sam and I froze midbite. The three of us gazed around the bustling cafeteria. Students ate, chatted, texted, did schoolwork, but . . . nothing happened. Sam and I slowly turn to Noah. Something had gone wrong.

Noah shrugged. "I don't know. It should've . . ."

Ding-ding.

High-pitched alerts sounded from everyone's phones, including Noah's and mine.

"Yeah, Amy would've timed that better," Noah admitted.

Along with everyone else, I pulled out my phone and saw the update alert on my screen. *Pop Chop update available*, it read, followed by *Update Now* or *Update Later*. I tapped the Update Now button and watched the progress bar fill as my phone downloaded the updated software.

And yes, I had gone ahead and paid to continue using the app. I didn't like the idea of giving money to the thief who stole my friend's app. But Noah and I agreed to pay in order to keep using it, and hopefully smoke out the bad guy.

"Look at all of them," Sam whispered.

I glanced up from my phone to see that I wasn't alone. Most everyone in the cafeteria stared at his or her phone as the update downloaded.

Sam grinned. "This is going to work."

Once the updated app was downloaded, it launched automatically. The loading screen appeared, followed by the main screen as usual. Then the unusual happened. A tiny string of computer code scrolled across the top of the screen before everything froze completely. I tried tapping the screen but nothing happened. I finally closed the app and then relaunched it. The sequence repeated itself before locking up again.

"That bit of code was a nice touch," I told Noah.

He smiled. "You like that?"

Sam leaned forward and scanned the crowd. "Okay, let's see who goes nuts."

There were plenty of displays of frustration going around the cafeteria, but nobody was going *nuts*. I would be frustrated too if I had just paid for an app I had been using for free, only for it to stop working because of some computer glitch. Honestly, we expected to see someone bolt out of the cafeteria or at least whip out his or her laptop. There was nothing like that.

"The thief must be somewhere else," I muttered.

"Okay," Sam sighed. "Plan B it is."

We put our trays away and quickly left the cafeteria.

Noah began with classrooms on the first floor while Sam and I bolted for the stairs. I got off on the second floor and she continued up toward the third.

Checking classrooms was easy. I peeked through each door window as I made my way down the hall. So far, all of them had been empty or had a teacher working behind his or her desk.

I had my money on the computer lab. Like Noah,

someone could access the developer site from one of the school computers.

I crept up to the lab and peeked inside. Sure enough, I wasn't disappointed. Three students were working inside.

At first, I wondered how I could sneak in without the perp seeing me. But then I remembered that if this was the app thief, he or she shouldn't be suspicious at this point. If Noah's plan worked, this person would merely think something went wrong in Amy's original code. They should just be anxious about trying to find the mistake.

I strolled through the door as if I had business there. Even though I was trying to act casual, I couldn't help but feel anxious myself. I was about to catch the app thief.

Two of the students, Ashley Robbins and Deena Bittick, sat near the front of the room, chatting more than working at the computers. They didn't seem flustered at all. I quickly ruled them out. That just left one person at the back of the lab.

As I drew closer, I recognized who it was: Anya Latke. Anya was an amazing programmer and already had a history of hacking. She was a hero to the students when she pranked the entire school with her *Cat*astrophe last year. She had hacked the school servers, and every school computer played nothing but cat videos for an hour. She could easily top the list of people able to pull off something like this.

As I moved in, she stared intently at the computer monitor. Her blond hair was pulled back, revealing a look of concentration. She didn't even look up as I approached.

I slipped my phone from my pocket and set it to camera mode. My plan was to walk by and sneak a photo of the app code on her computer screen. If we had solid proof, Mr. Davenport was bound to let Amy off the hook.

I closed in, raised my phone, and then . . . saw that she was watching—you guessed it—more cat videos. What was up with her and those things? Maybe she was gearing up for *Cat*astrophe II or a *Cat*mageddon. Either way, she was innocent—well, from hijacking the app, at least.

I swung around and headed toward the door when I received a text from Sam. **I got him,** it read. **And he's mad.**

I froze just inside the classroom. Sam sent a photo next. I enlarged the image showing Jamal Watts sitting at a worktable in the robotics classroom. Sam's photo caught him midsnarl as he stared down at his open laptop. His hands were on either side of his head in total frustration. It looked as if he was actually about to pull out clumps of hair. Lines of computer code filled his computer screen. I couldn't make out the blurry code in the image, but Jamal's frustrated body language said it all.

He was the app thief.

14

The Identity Inaccuracy

AFTER A FLURRY OF TEXTS BETWEEN THE THREE of us, Sam, Noah, and I decided to wait to confront Jamal. We had robotics class with him that afternoon, so we would do it there, in front of several witnesses. Sam thought it would help Amy's case if there were students other than Amy's three best friends to validate the story.

Time seemed to drag on as I sat through two more classes. There was only one more pop quiz, but since the app was down, the student grumblings were particularly noticeable. Everyone seemed to miss their early-warning system, especially since they had just shelled out some money to keep the privilege.

When I finally got to robotics class, Noah and Sam were already there. They sat at our worktable with the Choppa taken apart before them. As I joined them, I saw Tony and Maggie working at their table, but there was no sign of Jamal.

Sam turned a screwdriver, adjusting one of our robot's ax heads. "Do you think we waited too long?"

"I know, right?" Noah agreed. He wiped down the side of our robot's outer shell. "If he went home early, we missed our chance."

"And possibly our deadline," I added.

Just then, Jamal swooped into class right before the bell rang. I relaxed a little as he joined his teammates at their table, but I was still tense. I wasn't looking forward to confronting anyone, especially a fellow classmate. I thought of Amy and how she had looked when she was suspended. That image strengthened my resolve.

Luckily, Mrs. Scott had done her best to resist the pop-quiz edict. And with our big battle coming up, most of our classes were about prepping our robots, with her drifting from team to team, offering advice and answering questions. This would be the perfect place to confront Jamal.

I glanced in Jamal's direction to see him setting up at the far end of their worktable. While his teammates made adjustments to their robot, Flailing Grade, Jamal opened up his laptop and began typing away. His brow furrowed as he stared at the screen.

I caught Noah's eye and gave him a nod. I glanced at Sam and she set down her screwdriver and stood from her stool. The three of us marched over to Jamal Watts.

Jamal was so entranced in his work that he didn't see us approach. We were almost on top of him before he looked up. When he saw us, his eyes widened and he slammed his computer shut. I caught a glimpse of the screen before it disappeared; it was full of computer code.

"What's up, guys?" Jamal asked nervously.

"Is everything all right, Jamal?" Sam asked. "You look a little worried."

"I'm . . . uh . . . fine," he replied.

Noah smiled at Sam. "He does look a little tense."

I nodded toward the table. "What are you working on?"

Jamal slid a protective hand onto his laptop. "Nothing."

Noah rubbed his chin. "I'm guessing he has a little code problem."

Jamal's eyes flashed. "How do you know about that?"

Wow, there it was. Caught in the act.

"Do you realize how much you've hurt one of the nicest, sweetest people I know?" Sam asked, pointing a finger at Jamal's face. "Amy was suspended because of you."

"Suspended?" asked Jamal. He glanced at Noah and me. "What is she talking about?"

It turns out that I didn't have to be so worried about confronting Jamal. Sam was doing a fine job by herself. I glanced around nervously as the rest of the class began taking notice.

"Why did you do it?" Sam growled. Jamal backed away as she stepped forward. "Was it just about the money?"

"What money?" ask Jamal. "Are you talking about the robot battle? Is there going to be prize money now?"

"There's no prize money," said Noah. "We're talking about the five bucks you started charging everyone last night."

"Don't forget the part where you can upload your test

108

paper," Sam added. She poked his chest. "*That's* what got her suspended."

Jamal held up both hands. "Wait. You think *I* created the Pop Chop app?"

"We know you didn't create it," Sam replied, her eyes narrowed. "You just hijacked it."

Jamal cocked his head. "Are you . . . are you talking about the crash? Because I had nothing to do with that."

Noah jutted a thumb at his chest. "No, *I* caused the crash."

"Okay, wait." Jamal shook his head in confusion. "Then what did I do again?"

Something wasn't right here. Why was Jamal asking about the robot battle? Sure, the teams talk a lot of trash, but surely he can't think that's what this is all about.

Jamal certainly acted guilty enough. But then there's the stuff about us thinking that he created the app. Either Jamal had a world-class poker face or we got the wrong guy.

I stepped between Jamal and my friends. "Hang on a minute." I pointed to Jamal's laptop. "Can we see what you're working on for a second?"

Jamal gave me a suspicious look. "Why?"

"I think it might clear some stuff up," I replied.

Jamal glared up at me and then at Sam and Noah. Finally, he sighed and opened his laptop. The three of us crowded the screen. It was filled with code, all right, but . . .

"Look, I'm not trying to rip you off or anything," Jamal explained. "I just thought your robot AI was a cool idea. I was trying to write something like it for our robot."

The lines of computer code on Jamal's screen weren't for the Pop Chop app at all. The text was open in a completely different software package and interface. I recognized it at once. It was the same software Noah used to program the AI for our robot.

Sam glanced at Noah and me. She winced. "Whoops?"

"Doesn't matter, though," Jamal continued. "There's a glitch somewhere and I can't get it to work."

"Aw, man," said Noah. "You could've asked me for help. It's not like we're keeping our code a secret."

Jamal waved his hand at the three of us. "Really? After all this?"

Normally, one of the great things about the Swift Academy was the sharing of information. If someone came up with a unique string of code, he or she would happily share it with the other students. It's how we learned to attack problems from different angles. And even though the robot battle was technically a competition, we would've shown our AI code to any team that was interested.

"I'm sorry, Jamal," I said. "We thought you were someone else."

We briefly explained what was going on and why we thought Jamal was the app thief. We owed him that much.

"What are we going to do?" asked Sam. "Search the school again for another frustrated programmer?"

Ding-ding.

Everyone's phones chimed at once. Along with everyone else in class, I pulled out my phone and checked the screen. The Pop Chop had another update available. A wave of approving murmurs washed over the class of students. I downloaded the update and the app restarted. Everything was working normally again.

I shook my head. "Looks like the programmer isn't frustrated anymore."

15

The Dialect Directive

"WHAT DO WE DO NOW?" SAM ASKED. "AMY'S counting on us to find this guy. Did we miss our only shot?"

"I don't know," I replied.

I was usually great at planning on the fly, instinctively overcoming obstacles as they hit. But with so much pressure on us finding the thief and clearing our friend's name, I was drawing a blank. I didn't see a last-minute clear path like I usually did. All I saw was the way Amy had looked in the library.

"Do you think we can pull off another app crash?" I asked Noah, falling back on our original plan.

"Sure, I guess. We don't really have time to do anything else," Noah replied. "But we won't be able to do that if the thief changed the password."

"I thought you made it look like Amy scheduled the update a long time ago," Sam said.

"I did," Noah replied. "I even mimicked her programming style. But if it were me, I would've changed the password."

"Yeah, but you're paranoid," I said.

Noah grinned. "Being paranoid keeps you from being hacked." Then his grin faded as he let out a big sigh. "Okay, now I have to do something extremely difficult." He turned to Jamal. "Can I borrow your laptop real quick?"

Jamal raised an eyebrow. "Really?"

"Look, I'm sorry, I'm sorry, I'm sorry," Noah pleaded.

"*We're* sorry," I added. Sam nodded in agreement.

Noah held up a finger. "And . . . I promise I'll help you with your glitch."

Jamal shook his head and slid the laptop over to Noah. That saved us a bunch of time running back to our lockers to get one of ours.

"Thanks," Noah said as he pulled up the web browser

and navigated to the app developer website. He found the log-in page, entered the password, and . . .

"We're in," he said. "The password's still the same!"

"Schedule another update crash," Sam suggested. "Maybe right before school is out."

"I can do that." Noah scrolled through the code.

Jamal leaned closer. "That's the Pop Chop code? Nice."

Noah nodded. "Yeah, Amy does good work." He stopped scrolling and pointed to a line of code. "This is where I added the glitch."

Jamal squinted at the screen. "I see where they fixed it. Kind of clunky. I can think of two simpler ways to solve the problem."

Noah chuckled. "I know, right? Not half as elegant as Amy's work."

I'm a decent enough programmer, but I've never had the natural skill or appreciation for it like Noah. Jamal seemed to be closer to Noah's level, the way they excitedly picked apart each line of code. I caught Sam's gaze. She smirked and rolled her eyes.

"So the person who hijacked the app added the pay option and the test-scanning feature?" Jamal asked.

"Sure did," Noah replied. "Amy just wanted a basic alert system."

"Go to those parts of the program," Jamal said eagerly. "I want to see how they wrote that code."

Noah began to scroll down the page but then froze. "I'm such an idiot," he said.

"What?" Sam asked.

Noah groaned and then scrolled through the code some more. "I'm so stupid."

"What is it?" I asked.

Noah shook his head as he scrolled faster and faster. "I'm the stupidest guy in the smart-person school."

"What?!" Sam, Jamal, and I asked.

Noah stopped and spun toward us. "Okay, you know how I said every programmer has a unique style?"

"Yeah?" I said.

"Well, we know exactly what new features this person added to Amy's app. I could have been comparing his or her specific code to different projects in the computer lab. Everyone's coding style is like their handwriting, dude. Everyone is different and distinctive." He turned back and scanned more lines of code. "Man, I could've figured out who it was by now."

"Well, we can stay late," Sam suggested. "Go over all the code in the computer lab." She glanced at me. "Tom and I don't have the eye for it like you two, but we could help."

"Yeah, Mr. Davenport gave us until tomorrow . . . ," I began. I stopped when Noah held up a finger.

"Wait," he said. He tapped on the screen. "I know this guy." He smiled and stretched up both arms. "I know who it is."

"What?" Sam asked. "Just like that?"

Jamal leaned forward. He pointed to a line of code on the screen. "Oh, yeah, me too."

"Really?" I asked.

"Oh yeah." Noah nodded. A smile stretched across his face. "I recognize his programming style. I know *exactly* who it is."

I grinned. "Then let's schedule one last Pop Chop update."

16

The Redistribution Solution

I PULLED BACK THE JOYSTICK ON THE CONTROLLER.
The Choppa backed away and just evaded Flailing
Grade's foam ball. We weren't all-out sparring this time.
Sam wasn't even controlling the axes. School had just
let out, and the gym was mostly deserted except for a
couple of students chatting in the bleachers. As before,
a few fencers practiced at the other end of the gym. On
our side of the gym, it was just Jamal and me controlling
the robots while Sam and Noah watched.

I made our robot charge Flailing Grade, and the
round robot spun out of the way in a graceful pirouette.

"Nice," I said.

"Thanks," Jamal replied.

Sam checked her phone. "Almost time."

As Flailing Grade moved closer, I backed our robot away. As a group, we shuffled along with the dancing robots, moving closer and closer to the other end of the gym.

"Here it goes," Noah announced, scanning his own phone. Then it chirped in his hand.

Ding-ding.

The mosquito ringtones echoed through the gym as the few others' phones went off, too.

"Halt!" called a voice from the fencers' side.

As we and the robots edged closer, I spotted the tall fencer lower his weapon and remove his mask. Michel Villa wore a look of disgust as he strode to the gym wall. He rummaged through a backpack and dug out his own phone. He tapped the screen and growled with frustration.

"Someone's not happy," Sam murmured.

Michel looked up and waved away the other fencers. "That is all for today. Go away now."

The other fencers packed up their gear and left as Michel scowled at his phone.

"Check it," Noah said, showing me his phone.

As before, the Pop Chop app announced an update was available. Noah agreed to the update and a progress bar slowly filled.

I caught a glimpse of Michel impatiently waiting for the same bar to fill on his phone.

Jamal and I continued to mock-spar our robots, all the while creeping closer to the fencer.

Noah waved his phone in my direction, and I glanced over. The loading screen appeared, followed by a brand-new screen Noah and Jamal had created. *Your fee has been refunded!* it read. *Test scanning option no longer available.*

"No, no, no!" Michel growled. He shoved his phone back into his backpack and pulled out a laptop. He slid down the wall and opened the computer.

"Get ready for some fireworks," Sam whispered as she followed us even closer.

Michel typed furiously on his keyboard, paused, then typed some more. "Come on," he grunted. "This can't be happening!"

Now only a few feet away, I parked our robot and lowered the controller. Sam, Noah, and Jamal joined me as I took a few more steps toward the frustrated fencer.

"Everything all right, Michel?" I asked.

He didn't look up from his computer. "What?"

"You look like you're having some trouble there," Sam added.

Michel slammed his laptop shut and slid it aside. "No. Everything is fine." He grabbed his foil and got to his feet. He assumed a fencing stance and began to practice some moves.

"I don't know, Tom," Noah said. "It looked as if he's having log-in issues, huh?"

"Yeah," I agreed. "It did look like that."

Michel froze. "What do you know of this?"

"Well," said Noah, "because I'm the one who changed the password. And not just by one digit this time."

"Don't forget deleting his programming and returning all the money he collected," Jamal added.

"Oh yeah," agreed Sam. "That, too."

Michel's face twisted in anger. "You did this?!" He stepped forward and aimed his foil in our direction.

We each took a step back.

"Okay, maybe we shouldn't confront the guy holding the sword," Noah suggested.

"Foil," Sam, Jamal, and I corrected him.

Noah had a point. Even though fencing foils had a rubber guard on their tips, fencers wore protective masks for a reason.

"You stole the app from Amy," Sam said fearlessly. "We just took it back."

"Amy," he sneered. "She asks for training but has to stop all the time." He pointed to his laptop. "All the time on the computer. Then I saw what she was working on and I realized she was sitting on a gold mine and did not know it. It is not my fault she was too stupid to realize it."

"Stupid?!" Sam asked, lunging forward. "She got suspended because of you!" Noah and I each grabbed an arm and held her back.

"Yes, stupid." He aimed his foil at us once more. "Now, here's what is to happen. You give me the password and then mind your own business."

"No, *here's* what's going to happen," I said. "You're going to tell Mr. Davenport what you did and clear Amy's name."

"Why would I do this thing?" Michel scoffed.

"Because we're going to tell him anyway?" Sam snarked.

"Yeah, it might be better for you if you admitted it yourself," Noah added.

Michel laughed. "Fine. Go and tell him. I will deny everything. If you deleted my programming, then you deleted your evidence. I bet you did not think of that, did you?"

We glanced at each other.

He waved us away. "Now go back to fighting with your silly robots and leave me alone."

"Well, we weren't really fighting these robots," I explained. "Otherwise they might have damaged my phone attached to the front there." I pointed to my phone zip-tied to one of the front axes. "You know, the one that's been recording us this whole time?" I smiled.

Michel raised his foil and pointed it directly at my face. "Delete that right now!"

I toggled the joystick and our robot backed away. Michel took a step closer and I pressed a button on the controller. The Choppa spun 180 degrees before speeding toward the exit.

"Give me that!" Michel lunged forward and snatched the controller from my hand. He jerked at the joysticks and mashed buttons, but the robot kept moving away.

"Oh, that's my onboard AI," Noah explained. "It's overridden the manual controls and is running a special escape route I programmed."

"Get to za Choppa!" our robot said as it zipped out the door and disappeared down the hallway.

I nodded to Noah. "Nice touch."

"Why, thank you," he replied.

"No!" Michel shouted as he sprinted after it.

The four of us took off after him.

We ran out of the gym and raced down the hallway. The few lingering students backed toward the walls as we trailed Michel and the robot.

The Choppa wasn't built for speed, but it already had a good head start on the fencer. By the time Michel closed the gap, our robot had turned a corner and darted toward the front office. It shot past Ms. Lane's desk and disappeared through Mr. Davenport's open doorway.

Michel skidded to a stop and we piled up behind him.

"Get to za Choppa!" our robot sounded from the office. "Get to za Choppa!"

"Hey!" cried Mr. Davenport's voice. "What is this?!"

He stomped out of the room. "Ms. Lane, what in the world . . . ?" He froze when he saw us.

"Mr. Davenport," I said, stepping forward. I rested a hand on Michel's shoulder. "Mr. Villa here has something he'd like to tell you."

17

The Popularity Singularity

WHAM!

The Choppa's ax head hammered onto the outer shell of the opposing robot.

"Good one, Sam!" I shouted over the roar of the cheering audience.

"Thanks!" She made a quick adjustment to her safety goggles before returning to her controller.

"Evasive maneuver delta," Noah ordered.

I pressed a button on my controller and Noah's AI kicked in. Our robot backed away two feet before whipping around in a U-turn. Once the maneuver was complete, the AI released control. Noah pulled back on his joystick and the robot backed toward the enemy. Sam controlled the rear ax and it came down toward the other robot. Unfortunately, the yellow robot scooted clear of the attack. The opposing AI took over in its own evasive maneuver.

The audience groaned at the near miss. The other robot spun around, gathering momentum for its flail.

That's right. Our first bout in Mrs. Scott's big robot battle had us up against our old sparring partner: Flailing Grade. This time, however, our plastic ax heads were replaced with our blunt metal ax-shaped hammers, and Flailing Grade sported a metal ball. It was robot clobbering time!

A small arena had been built atop the gym floor for the contest. Clear plastic panels protected the operators as well as the audience in the bleachers. Our team controlled our robot from one side while Jamal's team stood on the other.

"This is amazing!" Amy shouted over the crowd. Our friend got a ringside seat right next to us. It was great to see her smiling again.

After Michel Villa's reluctant confession to Mr.

Davenport, Amy's suspension was lifted. Michel was suspended in her place, awaiting a full investigation. Things didn't look good for him, though. Our principal seemed just as upset once he heard that Villa had hacked a fellow student's program. If I had to guess, Michel would be heading back to France very soon.

"Yo, Amy! What's up?" Kevin Ryan asked as he walked past with his crew. The rest of his team waved to her as they brought their robot to the staging area.

Amy looked down and gave a quick wave. She had trouble getting used to her new popularity. See, it didn't take long for it to get around school that Amy was behind the Pop Chop app in the first place. All that *and* making the fencing team? She was a bigger hero than Anya Latke. Even though her last update had deleted the app from everyone's phones, the Swift Academy students were grateful for her help against the pop quizzes.

Unfortunately, there was a rumor circulating that I was the one who talked Mr. Davenport into giving up his pop quiz program. I tried my best to dispel that rumor (even if it was sort of true), but I think Noah was feeding the flames as quickly as I put them out.

He got no end of joy watching my fumbling reactions when other students asked me to get them more vegan options on the lunch menu or similar requests. Now I'd have to work twice as hard to be seen as just a regular student, even if my name was on the school.

Luckily, with the pop quizzes gone, we were able to spend more time on the Choppa. And we made *quite* a few upgrades.

"You with us, Tom?" Noah asked. "Let's stop that momentum!"

"You sure?" I asked. "Will the shielding take the hit?"

"It will," confirmed Sam. "You watch. The crumple zones will work."

"Nothing like a full-blown field test," I said, diverting power to the main motor.

Noah sped our robot forward, heading straight toward our spinning opponent. At the last second, he veered it to the left in a sideswipe. The tiny wrecking ball slammed into the side of the Choppa, denting its right panel. Noah rotated the robot toward Flailing Grade. The Choppa's motherboard was undamaged; we still had complete control.

"Told you," Sam said.

"Let's flip some burgers," Noah announced.

He rammed the robot at Flailing Grade before it could get up to speed. Once the ax heads slipped under the other robot, I adjusted the power levels. Now it was Sam's turn. She hit a switch and both axes shot up. Flailing Grade caught air and tumbled overhead.

"Beta! Beta!" Noah shouted.

I pressed the button for evasive maneuver beta. The power levels adjusted automatically as the AI kicked in. Our robot shot forward, zipping *under* the flipping robot. When it was clear, our robot skidded to a stop and spun around like a car from *The Fast and the Furious*. Flailing Grade slammed to the ground, bouncing onto its back.

The audience erupted in response to our fancy move.

Meanwhile, Flailing Grade tried to use its flail to right itself. Jamal and his team tried their best but they couldn't make it happen. They finally shook their heads in defeat.

"Winner by incapacitation!" Mrs. Scott's voice boomed over the PA system. "The Choppa moves on to the next round!"

The crowd applauded and cheered louder.

"Yes!" Sam shouted.

"Woo-hoo!" yelled Amy.

Noah and I bumped fists. He grinned widely. "You forgetting something?" he asked.

I shook my head. "Not at all." I pressed a button on my controller.

"Get to za Choppa! Get to za Choppa!" sounded from our robot. It was barely audible over the cheering crowd.

DON'T MISS TOM'S NEXT ADVENTURE!

- Restricted Access -

The Interrogation
Frustration

I PADDED DOWN THE STAIRS AS QUIETLY AS possible. I slid one hand down the handrail with the other steadying the backpack slung over my shoulder. I tried to keep my school supplies from rattling, a sound that might give away my position. Luckily, school was already out for the day, and I didn't run into any other students along the way. I'm sure I looked as if I was up to something—which I was, of course.

When I reached the first floor, I peeked into the main hallway. Only a few students were in sight. A couple milled by lockers and one shuffled toward the front door. There was no sign of *him*, though.

I took a deep breath and stepped out. I kept a brisk but quiet pace as I made my way to the center of the building. Once at the main intersection, I could turn left toward the front entrance or I could turn right and head out through the back door. My plan, such as it was, was to take a right.

I mentally kicked myself for not coming up with a real plan. Instead of waiting behind in Engineering class, it would've been so much easier to leave after the final bell rang. Then I could simply blend in with the crowd of exiting students. Now I was out in the open, exposed.

As I neared the main junction, I could see into the hallway leading to the front entrance. I skidded to a stop.

There he was. Inside the school.

The tall man wore a dark blue blazer and jeans. His back was to me as he peered into the chess team's trophy case.

I exhaled and slowly began moving again. I shuffled down the corridor toward him. If I could just make it to the junction without being spotted, I could turn right and duck out through the back doors. Unfortunately, he must have spotted my reflection in the glass case. The man spun around as soon as I was near.

"Tom!" He held up a hand. His gray-speckled beard stretched across his face as he grinned.

I nodded and sighed. I hitched up my backpack, gave a weak smile, and walked over to him.

"Sorry." I jutted a thumb back down the hall. "I was just . . . uh . . ."

"It doesn't matter, you're here now," said Mr. Kavner. He ushered me toward the front door. "Let's sit on the front steps. Get some air."

Steven Kavner was a friend of my father's. Normally, not someone I'd want to avoid. But he was also a journalist who wanted to interview me for a story. *That* was something that I wish I could avoid.

Mr. Kavner and I sat on one of the long cement steps. "State your name, please," he said.

I cocked my head a little. "But . . . you already know my name."

Mr. Kavner grinned. He tapped the tiny body cam poking out of the front pocket on his blue blazer. "Yeah, but just for the record."

I sighed. "Tom Swift Junior."

"Great," said Mr. Kavner. "And where do you go to school?"

I glanced up at the school's name stretching across the building above us. He just pointed to the small camera again.

"The Swift Academy of Science and Technology," I replied.

Mr. Kavner nodded. "Tell me a little about your school."

I squirmed a bit and sighed again. "Well, it's a special school where we get to learn advanced subjects, create our own inventions, and go on cool field trips. Stuff like that."

I knew I was really underselling it. The academy was way more than that. Advanced subjects? How about aerodynamics and engineering to go along with algebra and history. Create our own inventions? It wouldn't be unusual to see robots or drones zipping through the halls. I would know; I piloted some of them. And as far as cool field trips were concerned, last year the eighth graders had a lock-in at the Wesley Observatory. Shandra Watts even discovered a comet.

Yeah, I knew my description didn't do the school justice, and Mr. Kavner knew it too. He rolled his eyes.

"Gee, Tom," he said with a wide grin. "I couldn't help but notice that you and your school share the same name."

I rubbed the back of my neck and shifted a bit on the hard step. "Yeah, my dad founded the school with the profits from his company, Swift Enterprises."

Of course, Mr. Kavner was well aware of this, too. After all, he and my father had gone to college together. They had even worked on some inventions together. But I guess somewhere along the way, Mr. Kavner's interests had changed. The only reason I had agreed to the interview was because he was a friend of my father's.

The thing is, I wasn't too thrilled sharing my name with the school. Don't get me wrong, I'm proud of my father and his accomplishments, especially the school. But all I've ever wanted was to be treated like any other student. And now I was the subject of a news story that would do the exact opposite.